To Joan,
May music always
bless your heart!
Love, Sinéad

Playing Each
Other Home

Sinéad Tyrone

NFB
Buffalo, New York

Copyright © 2022 Sinéad Tyrone
Printed in the United States of America

Playing Each Other Home/ Tyrone 1st Edition

ISBN: 978-1-953610-26-3

1.Title 2. Fiction. 3. Music. 4. Literarture

NFB
NFB Publishing/Amelia Press
119 Dorchester Road
Buffalo, New York 14213

For more information visit Nfbpublishing.com

Also by Sinéad Tyrone

Fiction

Walking Through The Mist

Crossing The Lough Between

The Space Between Notes (combined fiction and poetry)

Poetry

Fragility

A Song Of Ireland

PLAYING EACH OTHER HOME

To Larry,

Thank you for always being
such a wonderful, supportive
cousin and friend.

1

Aidan O'Connell grabbed two mugs of steaming hot coffee and a bag with four buttered rolls and hurried out to the bench where Niall Donoghue sat waiting. Set at the dividing line between their two properties, the bench overlooked the pond where they both had swam and boated over the past few years, the house Aidan had bought a few years earlier and carriage house Aidan had converted to a music studio, and the sheep farm Niall's family owned. After a week of spring rains, the mid-morning sun shining down on them felt welcome.

"Took you long enough," Niall teased as he relieved Aidan of one of the coffee mugs. "I was just about ready to head back inside."

Aidan settled into the empty side of the bench. "Sorry. Mack called while I was brewing our coffee."

"He called me earlier. Teleconference tomorrow morning to discuss summer plans, right?"

"Aye." Aidan handed Niall one of the buttered rolls.

"It will be great to get back to work, even though you lot drive me crazy!" Niall took a long drink of his hot coffee, grateful for its rich warmth. The sun, though appealing to look at, did little to shake off the damp chill that still permeated the air. "I have to admit, though, the break was nice."

"Three months did give us all a chance to clear our minds

and rest our bones." Aidan nodded toward the new room extending off the back of the Donoghues' house. "You made good use of your time, getting that built."

Niall turned his eyes to the old stone and clapboard farmhouse he'd grown up in, surrounded by pastureland dotted with numerous white cloud clusters of his family's sheep, and the barn where he and his father worked each day. He watched his father emerge from the barn now, cross the yard to where his mother hung fresh washed laundry out to dry and exchange a few words with her.

"It was time," Niall told Aidan. "My parents have needed a downstairs bedroom these past couple of years. My father's last bout of cancer left him weaker than ever. I know he'll get some of his strength back, but it was an eye opener sure as the future was staring us in the face. Having a downstairs bedroom and bath will make their lives that much easier instead of having to drag themselves up and down the stairs all the time."

"Your parents raised a wise son."

"I do my best." Niall watched his father trudge back to their barn, taking in how the elder Donoghue's gait had lost its bounce, how his steps were shorter and slower. "I'm thinking this summer I should hire an extra hand to help my Da with some of the chores the farm demands."

"Your father will not agree to that!"

"He'll put up a fuss, sure; I'll just have to ease him into it."

Aidan fell quiet, as he sometimes did when thoughts of his own parents crowded his mind: his mother, beautiful and golden, who had died when he was young, and his father, strong and wise, who'd passed just a few short years ago along with Aidan's grandmother and sister. Niall and his family had all but adopted Aidan, integrating him into their lives as easily as a new branch is grafted onto a tree, but they could never replace the family he'd lost. Not a day went by when he didn't miss them. Sometimes, like now, his longing for them rolled over him like a black cloud blotting out the sun.

Niall could read Aidan's mind and the forlorn expression on his face. At times he would draw out the feelings and thoughts Aidan held close. Today, with the conversation bringing up his own fears for what the future might hold for his father, Niall chose to leave both of their emotions buried below the surface and changed the subject.

"Is Fionna home this weekend?"

Aidan shook his head. "No, she's still in Dublin. Her art show has another two weeks to go. She thought she'd take a run home tomorrow, but a couple of important art critics are coming in Saturday so she's staying out there. She's that nervous about trying to impress them."

"She's showing the same paintings she displayed in Belfast back in November, isn't she? Pauline and I thought they were stunning."

"Yes, most of the same ones. She added a couple of new pieces, one of Slieve League and one of the ocean at Malin Head."

"I remember her showing us the Malin Head one. The critics will love it."

"I don't know. You've seen how it is with our music; you can never predict what people are going to like. We look at her paintings and see beautiful images. Critics see depth and brush strokes, technique, proportion, a dozen details we aren't even cognizant of. Fionna's had showings I was sure would be winners, and the critics have cut her in two."

Niall remembered then how despondent Fionna had been after the critics panned her Belfast show, how she was sure her dream of success was over, how for days Aidan had been unable to convince her to pick up her brushes and paints and start over. "It's hard following dreams. We were lucky Mack found us and brought us together. I doubt we would have had the success we have without him."

"Too right." Aidan turned to view his house and studio. "I wouldn't have all this without Mack. And I best get back to organizing my studio so we can rehearse there again."

Niall finished his coffee and the second roll, then returned to the barn he'd spent the early morning cleaning and found his father trying to drag a metal gate from where it had been stored by a wall in the barn to the pen where, the day before, he'd helped Niall remove a rusted gate. "What are you trying to do there, Da? I told you I'd help you with that."

"I know you did. I just thought I'd get a head start on it."

Niall took hold of the free end of the gate and pulled it away from his father. "I'll take that part over now. Why don't you check our supply of supplements and make a list of what we need so I can place an order this afternoon."

Will Donoghue dropped his end of the gate, letting it clatter against the barn's cement floor. Niall could tell by the set of his father's jaw and stiff shoulders the man was none too happy to have been relieved of a job he'd once handled with ease. It couldn't be helped. He'd not have his father hurt himself doing more strenuous work than he was fit for at the moment. Maybe in time the man would have his strength back. Maybe, if there was time. The thought that there might not be struck Niall hard, as if the barn roof had collapsed down upon him. Out of the corner of his eye he watched his father lift various boxes and bottles, gauge their weight, then set each one down hard. He knew his father's mood would clear in time. For now, he'd just stay out of the way and focus on the task at hand.

Aidan brewed another hot drink, tea this time, letting it steep long until it was the color of peat, then carried it out to the studio where over the past few years he'd installed a mixing board, sound monitors, microphones and stands, chairs, and a leather sofa for relaxing on in between songs. Macready's Bridge had recorded their last album here; Mack had been so pleased with the quality he'd started spreading the word to other musicians. Last month a solo artist from Antrim had called asking about recording at the studio; while that booking had not yet materialized, Aidan felt sure his studio's reputation and business would grow. For the second time that morning he thought of his father, this time raising his eyes heavenward. "We did it, Da. Your dream of Roisin Studios is now real."

In the silence around him Aidan thought he could hear a whisper, "Well done." Sure it was only his imagination, he took comfort in the words anyway, believing his father and his family did look over him from time to time.

He opened the carton of sound proofing panels he'd received the day before and set about laying out and installing them. While the Macready's Bridge album they'd last recorded there was good, he had picked up on a slight, almost imperceptible background buzz in two or three spots. Installing these panels would eliminate any residual background noise and make his studio a more viable recording outlet going forward.

Returning to his house mid-afternoon, Aidan checked the mail he'd received in the morning's post: two bills, one envelope addressed to occupant, and one annual notice from his bank, nothing that needed immediate attention. He placed the mail on his desk in the study he'd created for himself in the back of his house, checked his mobile phone for messages, and saw he'd missed a call from Fionna. He rang her back right away.

"I'm sorry I missed your call. I was caught up working on the studio. How's the show going?"

"I don't know. I don't know if I've chosen the right pieces to hang. I should have brought the one I did of the flower stall on O'Connell Street. I should have included more Dublin cityscape pieces. I should have …".

"Whoa!" Aidan broke in. "You're panicking! Take a deep breath and shift your focus. The show's been underway two weeks already and you've had positive feedback so far, haven't you?"

"Yes," Fionna agreed, "so far the overall reception has been good."

"There you are, then. You're just nervous because of the critics coming in."

"I know I am." Fionna closed her eyes and inhaled several deep breaths, struggling to maintain composure. "Are you sure you can't be here this weekend?"

"I thought about it, but Mack's called a teleconference for tomorrow. There's no telling how long that will take."

Fionna had grown used to the conflict in schedules she and Aidan both faced. Ever since they'd started dating, they'd faced one challenge after another trying to combine her art classes and occasional displays and his gigs around Ireland, Scotland, England, and America. "I understand. I'll be okay," she told him now, not feeling okay at all, feeling anything but okay. She'd come to rely on Aidan's input, perhaps too much. She thought back on the independence and self confidence she'd developed as she had defied her parents' desires for her to enter librarian courses and instead pursued an art career, as she'd navigated art school and accommodations in Dublin, and started submitting her works to various galleries. Living with Aidan, she'd lost so much of her independent edge that now, when she needed self confidence most, instead of finding courage within herself she turned to Aidan and was left scrambling inside her learning he would not be there.

"Aidan would be here if he could," she told herself now. "You've got to believe in yourself."

After their call ended Aidan felt hollow inside, as he did whenever Fionna was away. He remembered the October day he'd asked her to move in with him; how she'd come up from Dublin for the weekend, how she'd cooked a delicious pork roast dinner for Aidan and herself and Niall and Pauline, moving with ease around the kitchen and dining room as if she had always worked in that kitchen, as if she'd belonged in the house, in his life, a natural fit. After dinner, after Niall and Pauline had left, as he'd helped her clean the kitchen and wash and dry dishes, he'd realized he was no longer content to just have Fionna over on occasion, but that he wanted her there all the time. Not quite ready to slip a ring on her finger and make a permanent commitment, he'd nonetheless asked her to move in with him, she'd agreed right away, and a week later had moved all her clothes and belongings in and taken up residence.

In the months since she'd moved in, Aidan had grown accustomed to Fionna's perfume filling the air throughout his house, the sound of her footsteps moving from room to room, her voice calling out to him or chatting on her phone with friends and art contacts, her singing along with her favorite music.

All the months before Fionna had moved in, Aidan had not felt the house was too empty. He'd accepted the silence as part of its features, the same as its walls, windows and floors. Now he knew the difference. Now the silence and emptiness throughout the house bore a heaviness that almost suffocated him. He wandered from room to room downstairs dissatisfied with his furniture choices, how he'd laid out each room, how bare the walls looked, until he realized it wasn't the rooms that dissatisfied him, it was his loneliness.

Returning to the living room, Aidan turned to Annie, his father's guitar, waiting as patient as ever in her corner. He lit a peat fire, less for the warmth it would fill the room with, more for the way the sight of it would lift his spirits, took Annie in hand, and played, with no agenda, no particular tune in mind, no words forming lyrics, just random music, and the sound of it all was so sweet to him it soothed like a gentle balm healing the aching areas of his soul.

Michael Sullivan sat back in the leather chair across from Diarmid Fitzsimmons, his peripheral vision taking in the mahogany paneling and gold records that lined the walls on both sides of the room while keeping his eyes focused on the man behind the desk. He still couldn't believe he was here, in the presence of Ireland's premier music producer, at the producer's request, with a chance of being signed on to the most prominent record label in the industry.

When Diarmid's assistant had called two days earlier to schedule a meeting, at first Michael had thought it was one of his friends pulling a prank. When he realized the call was legitimate, he was so nervous he could barely breathe or speak.

Now he had to force his mind to focus not on the luxurious surroundings of the room, but on the words Diarmid Fitzsimmons was speaking.

"I've followed your work for a while now," Diarmid was saying. "I'm very impressed with your voice and your style. I'd like you to come work for me."

Michael couldn't count how many years he had dreamed of

hearing those words from someone of Diarmid's stature. Why, then, was his mind now consumed with thoughts of Mack and Macready's Bridge?

"I'd be very interested," Michael replied, "but you know I'm in a band at present."

Diarmid rested his hands, fingers laced, on his desk. He'd been through this before with singers he wanted to sign up. Why did they always make it harder than it needed to be?

"I know what your status is. I also believe there's a solo artist inside you desperate to be released."

"I won't deny that," Michael admitted, amazed that Diarmid could have seen straight through to his deepest dream.

"Michael, anyone can have dreams, but only those with courage make them come true." Diarmid paused, giving Michael a moment for those words to register. "Do you have the courage to take that brave step?"

Courage, Michael knew, had gotten him this far along. Stepping out and singing at all, defying his father's wishes that he choose a more stable, success-oriented business career, had not been easy.

He'd thought Macready's Bridge had been the fulfillment of his dream. Now here was Diarmid Fitzsimmons offering the highest dream he could ever imagine.

Did he have enough courage left to take one more grand risk?

"I need to talk to my manager, Mack. I owe him a conversation about this before I make my decision."

"Of course." Diarmid rose and shook Michael's hand. "Let me know within a week what you decide."

He was still trying to decide if leaving the band and striking out on his own, albeit under Diarmid Fitzsimmons' umbrella, was the right course of action when he walked through the door of the house he and Susannah had bought the previous autumn.

"How did your meeting go?" Susannah asked, taking his wet raincoat and hanging it on a coat rack in the corner of their front room.

"He's offered me a contract as a solo artist."

"Michael, that's wonderful! What did you tell him?"

"I told him I need to think on it."

"That would be a terrible opportunity to throw away."

Michael studied the coffee table in front of the sofa where he'd sat down, taking in its clean straight lines, the smoothness of the glass inlay, the even spacing in the wood grain pattern, the rich deep brown of the wood. How sleek and smooth it looked, he thought, and wished life was as easily fashioned. "I never said I was throwing it away," he spoke after a long minute.

Susannah had learned over the past few years when to push her husband and when to step back and allow him space to sort things out on his own. She could tell by the way his eyes were focused on the coffee table in front of them rather than on her that he needed that space now. "You have a lot to think on," she told him. "I have some work to finish. I'll leave you to it."

So much to think on, Michael agreed. A solo career had been what he'd dreamed of ever since he was young, watching other singers do what his heart yearned for. He'd worked for that dream, taking every gig that came his way, seeking out new ones wherever he could, agonizing at times over how dry the well of possibilities could be. He'd been close to giving up when Mack Macready came upon him and offered him the chance to work in a group setting. Macready's Bridge had been a true blessing. While no longer solo, he'd been able to realize his dream of singing for a career.

Now Diarmid Fitzsimmons was handing him his original dream; but the only way to follow that dream would be to step away from the band he loved, from musicians who'd grown to become as close as brothers to him. And what would his leaving mean for the rest of them?

While Susannah worked, Michael wandered from room to room in their two-story house. He admired the kitchen with its brown and tan granite counters and stainless steel appliances, the living room where they had entertained family and friends, the dining room, site of so many dinners and game nights, and the office Susannah had set up to conduct her event planning business. Upstairs, he walked through the bedrooms, from the master bedroom Susannah had decorated with warm tans and greens, and the guest bedroom their parents had made use of several times. Last, he stepped into the small alcove bedroom Susannah had earmarked as a nursery in hopes they would someday have a baby. This last room gave him the greatest pause. If he agreed to Diarmid Fitzsimmons's offer, would it come at the expense of Susannah's dream should he fail?

"Don't you do that," Susannah ordered as he asked her about this over dinner. "Don't let hope of a baby of ours be the thing that holds you back right now. If you did that, you'd end up hating our baby, and even hating me. The only thing you should focus on is whether this offer is right for you. Everything else, either way, will work out."

Michael knew she was right, just as he'd known all afternoon, ever since receiving Dairmid's offer, what his decision would be. Before contacting Diarmid, though, he had one more call to make. After dinner, he dialed Mack's number.

"Mack, I received your message about tomorrow. I don't think I should participate."

Mack was surprised. It was not like Michael to ever miss a meeting. "Is everything okay?"

"It is. I mean, no one's sick, we're all fine." Michael dreaded saying the next words, but there was no other option. "Diarmid Fitzsimmons met with me today. He wants to sign me on as a solo artist."

Caught off guard, Mack was too stunned at first to respond. When he recovered, he told Michael, "I'm not surprised. I've told you all along how talented you are."

"I think I have to take him up on his offer." There. He'd said it. The knot in Michael's stomach loosened a degree now that the deed was done. "I don't think I can pass this chance up."

"You'd be a fool to turn him down."

"That's what I think as well."

"You could still be in on the call, tell the others yourself about your news."

"Thank you, but you have business to work out with the boys and I'll have plenty to do myself."

"Understood. I wish you great success with Diarmid. He can be quite hard on people sometimes; don't let him push you around. Stick up for yourself when you have to. And keep in touch, will you? I'm always around if you ever need or want to talk."

Mack turned to Kate after Michael had hung up. "We're losing Michael."

Kate set a fresh cup of tea in front of Mack. "I heard. What are your thoughts about that?"

"Michael was the hardest to get to know when I first organized Macready's Bridge. He was so much a closed book. He's always been a hard worker, dedicated to his craft. The more he's loosened up with us all, the more I've enjoyed his humor and the close bond we've all formed with him. I'll miss him very much."

"I heard you tell him Diarmid can be tough. Do you think Michael will be okay?"

A laugh escaped Mack's lips. "Kate, love, you sound like a protective mother hen! Michael's smart. He should be fine."

"What will you do for the rest of the boys? How will they all get on without Michael?"

Mack shook his head. "I haven't a clue," he admitted, staring into the clear, dark liquid in his tea mug as if the answer could be found there. "It will be hard enough telling them our summer schedule has changed. They can take that in stride; but they'll have to decide if they even want to move on without Michael. If they do, we'd have to find a new singer."

If Mack ever felt old the past few years, working to oversee Macready's Bridge's recordings and bookings, first across Ireland and Northern Ireland, then throughout America, and most recently in England and Scotland, he felt well past his years now with the new challenges the band faced. "Maybe it's time I gave up," he told Kate. "Maybe they all need a new manager who can fight better for them."

Kate rose from her seat across Mack at the small table in the breakfast nook of their kitchen, walked over to his side of the table, and wrapped an arm around his shoulder. "You love those boys, Mack, and they love you back. They wouldn't be happy working for anyone else. You'll feel better after your meeting tomorrow."

For a minute, Mack didn't move or respond, reveling in the feel of Kate's arm around him, the scent of her perfume, the comfort she offered even though in his heart he knew he and Macready's Bridge faced an uphill battle. Then he rose, drained his tea mug, and set their tea and dinner dishes on the kitchen counter.

"We'd best get the house picked up! Patrick and Moira will be back from their holiday in an hour or two."

Kate's eyes lit up the way they always did when Patrick and Moira and their children were around. In the few short years since Patrick and Moira had moved in with Kate and Mack after the premature birth of the Leahys' twins, Kate had relished her role as "Aunt Kate", enjoyed feeding and changing young Eamon and Eileen, and playing with Conor and Caitlyn, the older twins, or helping them with homework when Moira was occupied with the younger two. Ever since Patrick and his family had moved in, at first so Kate and Mack could help with the overwhelmed new parents, and then as the Leahy cottage seemed too small and Kate and Mack had much more room than they needed, they had all fallen into an easy routine, and now could not imagine any other living arrangements.

By the time Patrick's family pulled into the driveway, Mack and Kate had cleaned the kitchen, picked up the papers and jackets they had left lying about the living room, and sorted, folded, and stored away the basket of laundry they'd ignored the better part of the day.

"Aunt Kate," Caitlyn called out, rushing to the older woman who wrapped her in a tight hug. "We had fun! Conor surfed, and I steered a sailboat!"

"Oh my!" Kate greeted her with enthusiasm. "I hope you have pictures for me to see later."

"Over tea before bed?"

Kate had grown to enjoy that tradition as much as Caitlyn and Conor did, a few quiet moments in which to shower a little special attention on them, a habit they'd started when Eamon and Eileen were first born and commanded so much of their parents' time. Conor and Caitlyn now looked forward their evening ritual as much as Kate did.

While Kate and Moira saw to the children, Patrick and Mack carried suitcases and assorted bags and strollers inside. "I don't know, Mack, all this baggage hardly makes a holiday worthwhile!"

"It does seem that way, doesn't it? I'm sure you enjoyed your time away, though. How is your cottage holding up?"

Patrick pictured once again the two-bedroom thatched cottage outside Sligo he and Moira had lived in for years. "The roof needs a wee bit of patching, and one of the windows is cracked, but it's doing well overall."

"I thought Kate and I might borrow the cottage for a couple of weeks someday. Would that be okay?"

"You can use it anytime. Moira and I owe you so much for all the help you've given us."

Mack set the last of the suitcases in the hallway. "You owe us nothing, it's our pleasure to help."

"Well, our cottage is yours anytime you want to use it." Patrick finished hanging kids' jackets in the front hallway closet.

Mack debated how much he should tell Patrick about the phone call he'd received from Michael. With all the bustle of Patrick and Moira settling their children and themselves back in after their holiday, Mack decided Michael's news could wait until morning.

"I enjoyed our holiday, but it's good to be back home," Moira slid next to Patrick in their king side bed and pulled clean sheets and their crisp white duvet over her. Bedtime, after all four of their kids had fallen asleep, was the only real chance they had to talk anymore.

Patrick confessed what had been preying on his mind all the way back from their holiday. "It's not really home though, is it?"

Moira propped herself up on one elbow, her full attention focused on Patrick. "Of course it is. Mack and Kate told us as much, our home for as long as we want to live here."

"They meant that more to help us get back on our feet after Eamon and Eileen were born. That was a few years ago. I think it's time we start planning on moving back to our cottage."

"Patrick, you know that place will be far too small for us all. Our four kids will never fit into one bedroom. And the house itself was too crowded even when it was only us three."

"We made out okay this past week, didn't we? We can build onto the cottage, add bedrooms, expand the downstairs as well." Patrick sat up, excitement over the plans he'd turned over and over in his mind during the drive home now spilling out. "You always did love that cottage; aren't you anxious to get back to it, especially after seeing it again?"

"The kind of plans you're talking about sound expensive."

"With the money the band should pull in with this year's summer tour, we should be able to start renovations, or take out a loan if we fall a bit short. We should be okay."

Moira settled back down, picturing in her mind the spacious room she and Patrick now occupied, the view of the ocean it offered by day, the sound of waves rolling in and out that lulled her to sleep when the weather was warm enough to leave windows open at night. She thought of the downstairs in Mack and Kate's house, how large and modern their kitchen was compared to the tiny one in her cottage, the dining room big enough for them all to share a meal together, the living room with its massive fireplace and soft, cozy chairs.

Patrick was right, of course, she admitted to herself. Mack and Kate had been more than generous with their time and their house, and she would never want to overstay the welcome they had extended. Still, the thought of leaving such luxury behind caused a sadness in Moira that she would never admit to Patrick.

"You'll see," Patrick whispered to Moira as they both drifted off to sleep. "We'll fix that cottage up to be a fine grand place, just like we dreamed when we first bought it."

2

Darkness fell early as winter shifted to spring, a thick black cloak wrapping itself around the stone fortress that stood atop a hill overlooking the Irish countryside. Outside, mists gathered over fields and streams creating a gossamer covering under which deer, badgers and hares hunted food, and warring parties progressed towards enemy territory. Sentries posted at evenly spaced intervals around the fortress walls kept close scrutiny over the fields spread before them lest any advancing parties should appear. Occasional calls of a stag or owl pierced the air around the fortress; at each call the sentries' awareness was heightened as they peered through the dark veil to discern whether the call was animal born, or a decoy from enemy forces.

Inside the central room of the fortress, women dined on what was left of venison and root vegetables, while men gathered around a small fire in the middle of the room, discussing recent battles won and their concerns for what lie ahead as feuding clans tailed them at every turn. Children long since tucked into bed slept in rooms set off to the sides of the great room, while servants cleared dishes from the men's earlier meal and tended small fires around the interior room's walls that illuminated the space with rose gold glows.

The clan's leader, some called him king, listened as the men's discussions grew more agitated, them feeling more and more frustrated at being so closely hemmed in. The king understood their frustrations; he'd felt the same concerns to the marrow of his bones, responsible as he was for the safety of the men, women, and children he was charged with protecting.

Tension filled the room. Provisions were dwindling, they would have to hunt more game the next day although warrior bands had tightened the circle around them. Worry gripped his heart like clenched fists gripping spears in battle. He could not let the clan read his fear, though. Grateful for the cover of night whose shadows masked the concerns etched across his face, as the men's conversation grew louder the king sought to diffuse their agitation.

He called for the clan's harpist. "Play something soothing," he ordered, "something to take the men's minds off their troubles."

Seating himself just off to the side of the gathered men, the young harpist struck an opening chord, then moved his fingers across his harp's strings with finesse, drawing light notes from the instrument, filling the central room of the fortress with melody enough to soothe the spirits of all inside, causing them to forget, if only for a few hours, the dangers that lie outside the fortress's walls.

Aidan woke from the dream energized with new inspiration. Ideas for the next Macready's Bridge album struck like a lightning bolt, flashing so fast through his mind he could not keep up with them all. Still only five in the morning, he couldn't wait to organize his ideas; he threw jeans and a shirt on and dashed downstairs.

An hour later he'd done enough research to have formulated a plan. He printed off a number of pages of information he'd collected, then sat in his study, guitar in hand, writing notes on the printed sheets as he converted an ancient Irish song to guitar, step one of his plan. Step two would be to add fiddle and pipe and develop a more modernized version of the tune. For that he would need Niall and Patrick's input.

Niall arrived at Aidan's several minutes before their teleconference call was scheduled to start. While they waited, Aidan described his dream.

"What do you think? Would this be a good basis for our next album?"

Niall matched Aidan's enthusiasm with his own. "It would indeed! A dream that vivid is a gift; it would be wrong to not act on it."

"I thought so too. I'll bring it up during our call and see if the others agree."

"Wish me luck," Mack whispered to Kate before he started his teleconference with Niall and Aidan. "This won't be an easy call." With a deep breath and a quick prayer, he joined Patrick in his office and started the video call.

"Thanks for making yourselves accessible on such short notice," he started the call with.

"First, Michael won't be here today. He called yesterday; he's had an offer from Diarmid Fitzsimmons to go solo." He turned to Patrick. "I didn't want to tell you last night, I thought it best to wait until I could tell you all at the same time."

The remaining three stared at Mack, stunned.

"Did he accept the offer?" Aidan asked, unable to grasp the idea that Michael would really leave them.

"Wouldn't you if you were in his shoes?"

Aidan answered Mack with a nod. "I guess I would."

Now Patrick understood why Mack had been so preoccupied during breakfast. "That would be a hard offer to turn down."

Niall agreed with Patrick. "Michael's always dreamed of a solo career. This is his golden opportunity. No matter how hard it might be for him to part ways with us, he'd have to go for it."

"That's right." Mack informed them, "I asked him if he'd like to take part in our call anyway and tell you himself, but he thought it best not to. I'm sure somewhere along the way he'll be in touch with each of you."

Mack gave them a few minutes to digest this first bit of

news, then announced the greater reason for the call. "Losing Michael isn't our only problem. This year we've been left out of some of the festivals we've done well at the past few years: Milwaukee, Kansas, and Dublin, Ohio. We can still book some of the smaller Irish festivals in America this summer, but we need to consider the costs of traveling versus the lower amount of revenue we'll take in at regional festivals as opposed to the major ones."

"How did we lose the larger fests?" Aidan wanted to know. "We've been successful for them, drawn in great crowds."

"Most festivals are anxious to book some of the new talent coming out of Ireland." Mack reminded them, "You were the new act everyone wanted a few years ago. You're still good, but you know in this business there's always someone right behind you poised to take over the lead."

Niall watched Mack's facial expressions, reading the mixture of sadness and frustration Mack displayed. Poor Mack, Niall thought, he always tries so hard for us. This is the first time he hasn't come through with what we want.

"I can't believe we're shut out of all three of the big ones." As soon as Patrick said this, he saw Mack stiffen, an involuntary reflex as if Mack himself were to blame. "I don't mean it's down to you, Mack," he added. "I don't doubt a word of what you're saying. I know you always do your best for us. I'm just surprised."

"Festival budgets are tightening," Mack offered as another reason they were shut out. "The organizers are stretched as far as they can go to hire the acts people want. Macready's Bridge still has a strong core following, but you've seen the figures the past several months. Record sales and streaming revenue are down. Not your fault, it's just how the industry is. You all know that. We can get a new album out, that helps some, but new groups are out all the time, some of them are shooting straight to the top, a number of them are especially exciting to Irish music followers, and those are the acts the festivals are signing up."

Aidan's mind whirled as he dissected and interpreted Mack's words for himself. "So, we're down to small festivals, our popularity is slipping, and now we're without Michael. That's where we're at, right?"

Mack had always been upfront with the band. As hard as it was to admit where they stood, there was no dancing around the truth now. "Yes, that's the status of things."

Silence fell as reality set in among the Macready's Bridge band. They had each seen the rise and fall of musicians around them, they knew the pitfalls of the industry they'd chosen to make their living in; but knowing it and seeing it happen to others was far different than experiencing a downfall firsthand themselves.

In a flash, Patrick saw his dream of expanding the cottage he and Moira loved so well crumble to dust. Even with the small savings they'd managed to build up, they'd never have enough to complete the job if Macready's Bridge had hit bottom.

Relieved that he'd already finished the addition to his parents' house, Niall knew he always had raising sheep to fall back on, although he wasn't ready for that yet. He still had the dream of music in him and did not want to give that up.

Aidan thought of his recording studio that he hoped would gain attention from other musicians as a reliable place to record. He knew someday the studio would be his primary business. Still, he wasn't ready to accept the idea that Macready's Bridge was folding.

"Mack, you're not saying we're through, are you?" He asked, disbelief spreading through him as he understood the full impact of their manager's words.

Mack did not give Aidan a fast answer. He took his time, weighing his words, knowing whatever he said now would steer the direction they chose. When he did answer, he left it as open ended as he could.

"We have a lot of things to consider. Do you want to do any of the regional festivals in America this summer? It would possibly cost more than you would take in, but the exposure is still valuable. Or do you want to limit this summer's work to Ireland, maybe England and Scotland as well? In either case, we would need to break in a new singer. Or do you want to let Macready's Bridge go at this point?"

Mack scanned the faces before him, each of them registering shock and uncertainty. The news he'd delivered was a lot to take in. Even he didn't know the right course for them to take. "You don't have to decide any of this right away. Take a few days to mull it over."

Patrick, Niall, and Aidan stared at each other. The thought of not working together was so unfathomable for a full minute they were left speechless. Then Aidan's mind cleared enough for him to have an answer.

"Mack, I know you said we should take some time and think over what we want to do, but I don't need time." The sweep of Aidan's hand took them all in. "I love working with Patrick and Niall. I don't want to give that up. Ever since you pulled us together we've had a tight bond between us. I can't believe Michael could find it so easy to walk away from us, but I know a solo career has been a dream of his, and of course he should take this chance. Do you have any thoughts yet who we would replace him with?"

Mack shook his head. "Not yet."

"Right. Well, of course touring America this summer is out. Without the big festivals we wouldn't see a profit. It's April now. If we could break in a new singer over the next month or so we could book some shows across Ireland, maybe England or Scotland as well. Speaking for myself, I think that's worth a try."

"I agree." Niall looked at Mack first, then Patrick, then back to Mack. "I don't want to lose what we've had. If we can find the right singer, there's no reason we can't keep going on. For now, couldn't Aidan handle the vocals?"

"Aidan could handle some songs, sure," Mack acknowledged, "but we need someone to fill that traditional Irish tenor role that Michael supplied."

Patrick took a more realistic view. "I'm all for trying, but I have to be honest. Our income has slowed down over the past few months. You all know that. We all have bills to pay, not just me with our children and their medical bills and all, but each of us. I say we give it a try, but if we don't have a good turnaround over the next few months we may have to . . .". He stopped, not wanting to speak the words that were plain to them all.

"Alright then," Mack agreed, relieved that they had chosen to try and stay together. Seeing them break apart would hurt more than he would ever let on to them. "I'll start scouting around for a singer I think would fit."

"Tell him your idea!" Niall spoke up before Mack ended their call.

To answer Mack and Patrick's inquisitive looks, Aidan explained, "I told Niall this morning about an idea I had for our next album. We all know there's a wealth of ancient Irish music that hasn't been tapped into. Some of it only exists in archival records. We could pull together an album of updated ancient songs, ones that haven't been covered by other acts. Most of them would be instrumental, we wouldn't need a singer. I don't mind doing the initial research for songs if you all are agreeable, then we can circle back to this and see if there's any value to the idea."

"I like the thought!" Patrick shared Aidan's enthusiasm.

"I do too." Niall looked to Mack for approval.

God love them, Mack thought, they won't give up even when things look darkest. "Do your research," Mack told Aidan. "We'll see where it leads."

"Niall told us about your band," Anna Donoghue mentioned that evening as she handed Aidan a plate of her shepherd's pie then reached for Niall's dish. "Michael leaving, and your summer tour canceled, that's hard luck. Will you be okay?"

Even if he wasn't sure, Aidan would not have worried Anna and Will. "I'll be fine. We all will be. We have ideas for new music, and Mack's looking to book some shows for us once he sorts out a new singer."

Later though, enjoying a pint with Niall back at his house, Aidan admitted, "I still can't believe today's turn of events."

"Neither can I." Niall tried to make light of the massive disappointment the morning had brought. "Guess I won't need to bring on an extra farm hand this summer." Changing the subject, he asked, "Have you heard anything yet from Fionna? How is her show going?"

"She texted earlier this evening that the critics had arrived. She's so nervous I swear she'll have a heart attack!"

"She needn't be, she's very talented, her pieces are stunning. They'll all give her high marks, sure."

"Her paintings are beautiful, indeed; but we've already discussed how critics pull her art apart, just like they do our music."

"She'll be fine all the same. When she's back home, let's you, me, Fionna and Pauline have a night on the town."

Patrick, Moira, Kate and Mack settled around the fireplace in Mack's spacious yet cozy living room. Kate poured fresh wine for them all and handed glasses around, while Mack stoked the fire and added another peat log to ward off the nighttime chill.

"I'm glad this day's over." Mack took his place next to Kate on the sofa and wrapped an arm around her shoulders. "I was not looking forward to delivering such hard news."

"None of it's your fault, Mack. We all know the industry; we never expected to ride the crest of the wave forever."

Moira squeezed Patrick's arm in a show of support.

"Thanks, Patrick, I appreciate that. I'm glad you all want to move forward if we can manage it."

Patrick's brain was tired. Ever since their teleconference, all he could think of was how he would provide for his family if the band fell apart. He'd have to go back to the cement quarry if they'd still have him, or find other work if the quarry had no openings. The labor market was hard these days; if he couldn't find a job, what then?

"There goes our cottage dream."

Not realizing he'd spoken his thoughts out loud, Patrick was stunned when Mack answered, "You and your family will always have a home here."

"I'm that grateful, we all are, but I had hoped we could get back to our own place in due time. No offense meant; you and Kate have been that kind to us when we needed help the most. Still, at some point Moira and I had hoped we could make our cottage suitable for the four kiddies and us and give you back your peace and quiet."

"Peace and quiet can be overrated." Kate thought of the children sleeping in their beds upstairs, of how much she enjoyed being "Aunt Kate" to them all, and tried to calm her fears of the day they would ever leave. "I understand you'd like to be on your own again someday. I'm sure that will happen in time, but don't ever think we don't love every minute of having you all here."

"Thanks. Alright, enough of that. Let's turn things to a positive light. Mack, it shouldn't be hard to find us a singer that would fit, should it?"

"It shouldn't be." Mack teased, "I found you lot, right?"

They laughed over Mack's statement, and a few more quips, before Patrick and Moira headed to bed, knowing they'd be up early in the morning with their children home schooling the older two and teaching numbers and letters to the younger ones.

Kate remained in front of the fireplace with Mack, watching the embers fade as the once vibrant burning logs themselves drifted off to sleep. She let peace settle over them a while before asking, "You're not sure at all about finding a new singer, are you?"

Mack listened to the soft crackling of the dying embers. "It shouldn't be hard. There's plenty of musicians to be had, I'll just have to scout around a bit." He wished inside he felt as confident as his words to Kate sounded. True, there were any number of musicians in Ireland looking for jobs. Finding the right one though, whose personality and style matched Aidan, Niall, and Patrick's chemistry, well, that might be a more difficult challenge.

3

Fionna's mind raced as her car drew closer to Aidan's house, the house she now called home. She'd gotten a later start than she'd planned; instead of arriving by lunch, it was now early evening, the sun had already started its descent toward the horizon and the hills she drove by wore their late day shadows. Excitement and dread mingled inside her as she debated how she would tell him her news.

As she drove, Sunday afternoon's turn of events replayed in her mind.

All her worries about the critics coming to see her art show that weekend had been for nothing. Each one had praised her works and given her high marks on composition, use of color, and techniques. If that had been all she'd received, it would have been enough.

Then Ed Kimbrough, one of the New York critics, had pulled her aside.

"I have an opportunity for you if you're interested," he'd announced, then proceeded to explain, "I'm associated with Gatewood Art Academy in New York City. The academy's next session starts the middle of May and runs through the end of August. One of the students we had signed up for this session has cancelled; we'd like to offer his spot to you."

Stunned at this unexpected offer, Fionna was speechless.

"You have great talent," Ed continued. "Our school can help you advance to the next level, if you're interested."

"I'd be very interested," Fionna told him. "I'd like to know more about the costs involved, and what the program offers."

"Of course. The program is a balanced schedule of in-class instruction geared towards sharpening and fine tuning an artist's skills, and free time for our students to draw, paint, sculpt, whatever their medium is. Our students also present their works at an end-of-session art show. On occasion, a student may be chosen for private showings to select clientele. We offer grants to cover the cost of the program, and we arrange accommodations. Your financial responsibility would only be for your meals, transportation, and personal expenses."

"That's quite an offer," Fionna responded, trying to grasp all the opportunity entailed. "Can I have a day or two to think it over?"

"Of course. We would need an answer by Wednesday, though, to ensure all your travel documents can be arranged, or to offer the spot to someone else if you can't accept."

"I understand; I'll call you by then." Fionna had promised.

Now, as Aidan's house came into view, Fionna's mind swirled faster.

New York City was a goal she thought would take years to reach. To have that door open now, no matter how slim the crack, was like a shot of adrenaline to her dreams. A dozen new ideas flooded her mind as she envisioned how she could capture the city's iconic streets, buildings, and parks on canvas. The end of session art show, possibly a private showing as well, and opportunities to network with additional American contacts was irresistible!

How she would break the news to Aidan was the only drawback.

They had both grown used to juggling their conflicting schedules, sometimes going weeks at a time without seeing each other. Once she had moved in with him, and with Macready's Bridge's bookings decreasing with summer over, they'd had more time together and had grown used to each other's constant presence. Aidan had even commented, the night before she'd left for her current Dublin art show, how much he enjoyed having her around, how empty the house would feel without her. Guessing he would not be thrilled with her news, Fionna resolved to tell him straight away. Putting it off would only make the telling harder.

Aidan wrapped her in a tight hug when she walked through the door. "I missed you! I know this is a short visit, but I'm so glad you're here."

If he noticed Fionna's return hug carried half the enthusiasm of his, Aidan did not mention it.

Fionna dropped her overnight bag by the sofa and sniffed at the aroma emanating from the kitchen. "What smells so good?"

"I tried to get salmon but the market in town had none, so I'm making roast beef instead." Aidan led Fionna into the kitchen to show her his efforts. "Do you think we should invite Niall and Pauline over for dinner?"

"No!"

At the sharpness of her response, Aidan's smile vanished.

"I'm sorry," Fionna apologized. "You know I love seeing them, but I have such a short time here and I need to discuss something with you."

"You said you did." Aidan recalled her phone call the night before. "It must be pretty important for you to make a quick run home like this."

"It is. It's something better discussed in person rather than over the phone."

Fear gripped Aidan as a dozen thoughts, and one in

particular, barreled through him. "Fionna, are you breaking up with me?"

The panicked look on Aidan's face almost caused Fionna to laugh. "What? No, of course not!"

Relieved, Aidan grabbed two bottles of water and led Fionna back out to the living room. "Alright," he said as he handed one of the bottles to her, "what's up?"

With no more time to debate her approach, Fionna was forced to plunge ahead, ready or not.

"I've been offered a chance to attend an art program in New York from mid-May to the end of August. Expenses will all be paid except for my food and travel. It's a fantastic opportunity to connect with the New York art community. I don't even know why I'm so nervous to tell you, you'll be away touring all summer anyway."

"No, I won't." At Fionna's surprised looked, Aidan explained, "Our festival gigs are out, we won't be going to America, and Michael's left the band, so I don't even know if we'll have any work at all this summer."

"What's happened with Michael?"

"He's going solo. Diarmid Fitzsimmons has lured him away."

"Oh, Aidan, I'm sorry."

Aidan waived off her apology. "It's not for you to worry about. New York? All summer? Wow."

Fionna caught the flat tone behind Aidan's words. "It's a grand opportunity for me, Aidan. I really think I should take it."

"You don't need my permission. Go ahead!"

"I know I don't, but you're my partner. I mean, I know we're not married, or engaged or anything, but we are living together and I didn't think I should make such a huge decision without talking it over with you first."

31

Truth be told, the thought of Fionna being away all summer scared Aidan. He couldn't even make it through two weeks without missing her so much he felt like a fisherman adrift on the ocean with a storm rolling in. How would he ever survive three months? Wrapped up in his own fear, Aidan almost missed what Fionna said next.

"Don't tell me what you think tonight. We should both sleep on it. I can make my decision tomorrow."

Michael reviewed once more the contract Diarmid Fitzsimmons had presented to him and, still awed that such fortune had come his way, signed the document.

"Welcome aboard!" Diarmid slid the signed paper into the side drawer of his desk. "Now, let's go over my plans for you."

Michael listened as Diarmid outlined a three-pronged approach to introducing him anew to a listening audience always eager for a fresh voice.

"First, we need to refine your image. I don't care if you wear jeans around the house, but when you're out in public I want you dressed in slacks and shirts, a suit when the occasion calls for it, and quality shoes. You need a new, more sophisticated hair style, and I don't ever want to see you out and about unshaven."

Michael held his tongue and didn't object to Diarmid's directives.

"You'll start receiving invitations for various social engagements. They're designed to keep you in the public eye. You may not be able to accept them all, but I would like to see you, or you and your wife, Susannah isn't it, at as many events as possible. These will be important both for photo op and networking aspects."

Diarmid pushed a fresh sheet of paper across the desk's

smooth mahogany surface towards Michael. "These are the songs I'd like you to start out with. It's a long list, not every song will appear on your debut album, but I'd like you to learn them all anyway."

The list Michael reviewed contained a mix of traditional Irish and contemporary American songs, some he was familiar with, some he'd never heard before.

"Can I ask a question? I'm an Irish singer. Why add so many American covers into the mix?"

Diarmid explained with the patience he'd developed over years of newbies asking the same question. "I understand you already have a fan base, but we're trying to broaden your appeal, draw new followers in. Choosing songs others are already familiar with will help build a wider audience for you, especially in America."

"He's got quite a comprehensive approach," Michael told Susannah over dinner that evening. "He's outlined everything, from new music to social engagements, even to the way I look."

"The way you look? What does he want to change?"

"Hair, clothes, the whole lot."

Susannah had to laugh. "Remember when I first met you and tried to get you to dress better, and you refused?"

Michael sighed, "I should have known you'd win in the end!"

"I always do!" Susannah passed a dish of roasted vegetables to Michael. "Will you be okay with all his demands? He's quite a change from Mack, isn't he?"

"He is indeed." Michael set the serving dish down, too deep in thought to bother with vegetables. "I'm sure I'll be fine working with Diarmid. As strict as he sounds, he knows the business and can get me where I want to go."

Fionna was still asleep when Aidan woke. In the shadows of the dim morning light entering their room, he watched her body rise and fall with her deep, even breaths, studied how smooth her skin looked, how a few stray strands of her copper hair danced across her cheek. So many mornings since she'd moved in he had hurried through these early morning moments, eager to get the day underway and accomplish the myriad tasks on his list. This morning he recognized the moment as the gift that it was, and absorbed the beauty of this quiet time, while she slept, before the demands of another day intruded.

Then he remembered Fionna's news. The idea of her being away all summer still shook him. Unable to relax any longer, Aidan dressed without waking her, and went downstairs.

He was on his second cup of coffee by the time she wandered down, showered and dressed in jeans and her favorite cream-colored sweater.

"Breakfast?" He offered and pulled out a frying pan without waiting for her reply. He cracked eggs into the pan, slipped sliced bread into the toaster, and poured orange juice for them both.

Fionna watched him work, noting his silence, feeling the tension that built up in the space between them, until she could not stand it anymore.

"You're very quiet this morning."

Aidan poured coffee and set it in front of her. "I have a lot on my mind."

"We both do." She kept her eyes on him while adding cream and sugar to her coffee.

Aidan buttered the toast, fixed two plates, and carried them both into the dining room. Fionna followed with juices and coffees.

"Are we going to talk about this?"

Aidan shook extra pepper over his eggs. "There's not much to talk about. You're going to New York."

"And you don't want me to go."

"Of course I do. It will be good for you."

"You don't mean a word you just said."

Aidan set his fork down harder than he needed to. "What do you want me to say? I know this is important to you, but I'd be lying if I said I didn't want you here this summer."

"But it would be different if I were home and you were away on tour, right?" Fionna challenged.

Aidan held his tongue, knowing she was right.

"Let me ask you something. Did you want me to move in here because you love me, or because you didn't want to be alone?"

"What kind of question is that?"

"An honest one." Fionna studied Aidan's face, and especially his eyes, noting his confusion, his inability to answer. "Aidan, you need to think that over, and make sure you know why you wanted me here. Why it would be okay for you to be away for a long stretch, but not for me? What is our relationship really about? I have some research to do before I head back to Dublin this afternoon. You should think about your answers while I work."

"This afternoon?" Aidan cast a sharp look at her. "I thought you were staying another night!"

Fionna looked straight at him, willing him to say the right words, begging inside for him to say what she wanted to hear, that he loved her, that he supported whatever she wanted to do. When those words didn't come, she told him, "I'm not sure there's a reason to."

Aidan stormed out to his studio, ignoring the breakfast

dishes that needed clearing. What the hell had just happened, he wondered. Not love her? Where did Fionna get her ideas? He threw his anger into his work, slamming boxes on the top of the table he'd installed, shoving chairs around, moving delicate equipment with more force than he should.

When he'd fully exhausted his anger, he sank into one of the chairs and thought over what Fionna said. This time, with a clearer mind, he had to admit her words held some truth. He did hate being alone. As much as he loved his house, as much as he knew Niall and the Donoghues were right across the field any time he wanted to be around people, too many nights the empty rooms in his house echoed his footsteps back to him, too many days the silence bore down on him like weights tied to his spirit, dragging him down.

Did he love Fionna, or did he just crave companionship? He was no longer sure. He did, though, know she was right about one thing. There was no difference between him heading off for a tour for months on end or her spending a summer in New York. He could no more try to talk her into giving up her dreams than he would allow her or anyone else to hold him back from his own.

"Fionna?" He called out when he returned to the house. "Can you come down here?"

When she appeared, he told her, "You were right this morning. I don't like being alone. I do love you, though. Is this Gatewood Art Academy offer that big of a deal?"

"Oh Aidan, it's a chance of a lifetime! I've researched the school quite a bit since yesterday. At the very least it's a chance to make good contacts, and the possibility of a private showing while I'm there would be a huge bonus."

As Fionna described the art academy, Aidan caught how her emerald eyes shone, how bright and animated her face was. He understood the thrill of following one's passion, of chasing a dream, and the incomparable joy of having a dream come true. He could not stand in the way of her reaching out for something so important to her.

"You've got to go for it. You don't need my permission, but you do have my support. And I love you."

From her dining room table workspace, Susannah could hear Michael in the room next to her, which doubled as an office for her event planning business files and and records and a place where Michael could study and practice his music. As she searched the internet for new venues and supply outlets, emailed contacts, and confirmed previously arranged plans, she could hear him play over and try to sing some of the songs from the list Diarmid had given him.

He'd explained to her how he was going through each song, the familiar ones as well as the ones newer to him, fixing them in his mind until they became such natural extensions of his thoughts that he could recall their words and melodies in an instant. After that, he'd told her, he could work with Diarmid's studio musicians to give each song a fresh treatment.

If the repetition of hearing each song over and over wore on her nerves, Susannah reminded herself where Michael's career had taken them over the past few years. From meeting and falling in love, to marriage, and then buying their own house in the Dublin outskirts, their lives were on a successful track. Now, with Diarmid Fitzsimmons lifting Michael to the next level, their greatest dreams were within reach.

Susannah rose and stretched her arms and legs. She'd sat at that table too long; moving around felt good. She walked a lap around their living room, then entered their kitchen where she poured two glasses of ice water, drank half of one, then carried the other to the office room.

She waited at the door until Michael had finished the song he was listening to, then knocked once and entered.

"You must be thirsty by now." Susannah handed Michael the fresh glass of water. "How is it coming along?"

"I'm getting a handle on the songs I'd never heard before." Michael set the water on the desk beside him. "Thanks. How is your business going?"

"Fine. I booked two new venues and have the catering sorted for another event."

Michael studied Susannah standing in front of him, noted how her face radiated joy, her eyes sparkled with excitement. "We're doing it, aren't we love? We're realizing all the dreams we ever had!"

"It's hard to believe, isn't it?"

"I keep pinching myself to make sure this new step up is real!" Michael thought of the morning he'd spent listening over and over to the same songs, the days behind him, the hard work ahead, and at the end of it all the prize, the soaring solo career he'd so long dreamed of. "There's still so much ahead, but it's all within our grasp."

"It is indeed! And I best let you get back to your work."

Before returning to her computer, Susannah tiptoed upstairs to their spare room, still cluttered with boxes from their move that they hadn't had time to sort through. In her mind's eye she imagined it decorated, not with the twin beds and dresser they'd originally planned, but with a fresh coat of paint, lemon yellow or pale mint green, with a white dresser and crib, and teddy bears stenciled along the walls. She prayed the change in Michael's career from band member to solo artist wouldn't interfere with their baby plans.

Fionna approached Dublin with a mixture of excitement and guilt.

She'd seen the fear in Aidan's eyes as she had pulled away from his house. He was still supportive of her going to New York, had told her as much over their early afternoon sandwiches and soup. He had been sincere in his support, she could tell. They both knew, though, her time in New York could change things for them both. It was the same fear she felt every time Aidan went out on tour, knowing he would meet any number of girls, wondering if he would still be interested in her when he came home.

Fionna remembered how much courage she had needed when she first went against her parents' desire that she build a career for herself in library sciences instead of following her pipe dream of making a living through art. They were unhappy with her for a while, but eventually came around as her art appeared in various galleries and she earned a modest income from sales.

She only wished she didn't have to go through so much angst, so much inner conflict, in following her dreams. Why couldn't the path be a little easier?

All during her drive back to the city she had weighed her options, not that there was any real choice. She knew artists and other dreamers fell into three categories: those who only dreamed but never found the courage to follow their dreams, those who followed their dreams, who took the first brave steps forward but only went halfway, too afraid of risk and failure to reach their highest goals, and those who pushed forward all the way, facing their fears, accepting the risks, reaching their highest potentials.

Fionna could refuse the offer she'd received, stay in Dublin, and accept that her works would be limited to regional or even national recognition but not go much beyond her island's borders, for the sake of not risking the relationship she was building with Aidan. Or she could accept the offer, pursue the next level of her dreams, and prove to Aidan that this would not interfere with the life they were planning any more than his many weeks and months on the road would.

Fionna knew the choice she had to make. As she drew near Dublin, she placed her call.

"Mr. Kimbrough? This is Fionna Fallon. Is the opening you mentioned still available?"

"Yes, I've held it for you."

"Wonderful. I'd love to accept your offer."

4

Pauline stared out the window at the rain cascading down, dripping like crystals from the roofline above her, creating silver white puddles across the fields beyond her parents' house. She tried to find beauty in the unique blessings rain brought, its soft patter on roof and windows, its nurturing of grasses and grains, how green the fields and other vegetation looked. Most days she could find the blessings in whatever the world presented to her. Today, though, she could find no beauty or joy.

Saturday chores called to her. She should be stripping beds and washing sheets, and dusting while her mother baked, but she found motivation hard to come by. Too many thoughts crowded her mind.

Niall had been quiet since his teleconference meeting with Mack and his Macready's Bridge mates. Since then, she had talked with him by phone enough to know that Michael had stepped away and the band was in need of a new singer, and that their summer tour in America was off. He had been so downcast by his turn of events she'd not been able to share her own news with him.

She couldn't put it off much longer, though.

Pauline had hoped she could convince Niall to break away from his work around the farm and go for a drive with her before she had to take her shift at the pub that evening. Rain was not conducive to an afternoon drive, though. She'd have to invent some other plan.

Her eyes fell on the fresh cinnamon rolls her mother had baked for their breakfast. "Mam, you don't mind if I take a few of these over to Niall, do ye now?" Without waiting for an answer, she tucked four of them into a box, grabbed the blue plaid wool shawl Niall had given her for Christmas, and was in her car pulling away before her mother could protest.

Niall's kiss when she caught up with him in his driveway was hurried, distracted. "I'm sorry love. I'm tied up here. If you'd called, I would have told you not to come round today."

Pauline read the urgency in Niall's eyes and in the movements of his parents hurrying around the barn and yard. "What's wrong?"

"Five of our lambs have come up lame. We're treating them for scald. We've a lot of work to do to treat them and make sure it doesn't spread to the rest of our sheep or grow worse."

"What can I do to help?"

"Nothing." Niall saw the hurt in Pauline's eyes. "I'm sorry. I can't take time now, my Da has his hands full. I need to get back to him."

Pauline knew scald, if not brought under control in short time, could turn into foot rot and threaten much of the Donoghues' flock. "I'd best let you get back to your work, Niall. Call me later." She set the box of cinnamon rolls on the steps leading to Niall's front door, and disinfected her boots while Niall sprayed disinfectant on the tires and lower portions of her car. "Don't forget to pick this up when you take a break."

Niall and his parents worked throughout the day. They examined their entire flock and found two more lambs and ewes which appeared to have scald. The entire flock was run through foot baths to prevent the scald from spreading. The lambs and ewes most affected were separated to a drier pasture. Niall then detailed the diagnosis and treatment for each sheep in the farm's journal.

It was well past dark before Niall and his parents sat down to dinner. Only then did he remember the box Pauline had left on their front step. He retrieved the box, opened it to find the cinnamon rolls, and set them in the center of their dinner table.

"I was pretty short with her," he admitted to his parents, recalling how he'd been so brusque with her earlier that day. "I barely gave her a minute of my time."

With a reassuring pat on his hand, Niall's mother told him, "I'm sure she understood. She knows what you were dealing with."

"Why don't you give her a call?" His father suggested. "I promise we'll save one of these rolls for you."

"You'll be saving two of them for me, or you'll get none at all!" Niall teased, pulling the box just out of his father's reach. Then he returned it to the table center, picked up his phone, and stepped outside for privacy.

"Hey, love, I just called to tell you I'm sorry I paid you so little mind earlier. Thank you for the cinnamon rolls, they're delicious!"

Pauline finished pulling a pint for one of the pub's patrons, then stepped back to talk to Niall. "You've got nothing to be sorry for. You had your hands full. Did you get everything sorted?"

"Aye. We've done the best we could. We'll have to monitor the rest for a while, but hopefully we've stopped it from spreading."

"I'm praying for you all."

"Thank you for that. I think we've caught it in time. Anyway, I wasn't expecting to see you today. Did you stop by just to deliver the baked goods, or was there something else on your mind?"

Something else on her mind? If only you knew, Pauline thought. She was desperate to tell him why she'd stopped by; but he had enough on his plate just now, and she didn't have the heart to add to his burdens. "No," she answered. "I just hadn't seen you for a bit and was missing you too much to wait any longer."

"I promise, as soon as we have our sheep under control I'll take you someplace special and make up for ignoring you the way I have."

Pauline went to bed that night no closer to resolving her problem. She prayed the Donoghues' sheep were cleared before it was too late to talk things over with Niall.

Larry Jaeger stared out the window of his Rochester, New York apartment to the expressway below. So many cars and trucks, he thought, all hurrying with business to conduct, people to meet, errands to run. He would be one of them if circumstances were normal, if anything in his life was normal.

Then again, if his life was as it should be, he would not be in this cramped city apartment looking out over the expressway and a dozen decaying buildings. He would be in his home in the country, with his wife, his fifteen year old daughter and twelve year old son. He would be on the road, transporting entertainers from one city to another on their tours, the job he'd worked for the past nine years, the best job he'd ever held.

Where had it all gone wrong? Larry couldn't pinpoint any one incident; it had been a buildup of many issues over the years, too many birthdays and holidays he was away for, too many crises his wife, Christine, had had to manage without him, too little meaningful communication between them to the point where any flame of love had long since burned itself out. As the calendar had turned from the old year to the new, Christine had turned a new page in her life and demanded a divorce.

Watching traffic flow below him now, Larry recalled Mack's phone call informing him Macready's Bridge would not need his driving services this summer. A cursory search showed a couple of possible driving positions available, but nothing desirable, nothing exciting.

Larry's phone ringing interrupted his thoughts. He recognized the international phone number and grabbed his phone before he lost the call. "Hello?"

"Larry? It's Aidan O'Connell checking in with you. How are you?"

Aidan's voice was just the tonic to lift Larry's spirits. "Hey, it's good to hear from you! Mack called the other day; I know your tour is off. I'll miss all of you this summer."

"We'll miss you as well. What are you going to do now your summer's freed up?"

"To be honest, I have no idea. I'm sure I could pick up some charter tours, but my heart's not really in it at the moment. You and the rest of the boys always made my summers more fun than anyone else I drove for."

"You always made it fun for us as well." Aidan could hear disappointment in Larry's voice, and something else. Depression? Frustration? Aidan wasn't sure what, but this wasn't the fun loving, easygoing Larry he was used to. "Hey, are you going to be okay?"

"Yeah." Larry tried to inject a lighter tone into his voice, if only to convince Aidan. "I'll be fine. It's just, my divorce has been finalized, my kids are getting older and spending most of their time with their mother and their friends so I don't get many visits in, and I'm just kind of at loose ends. Once I figure out what to do with my summer I'll be okay."

Aidan recalled conversations he and Larry had held in the past in which Larry had expressed some of the problems he and his wife were going through, and later that they'd filed for divorce. Knowing their favorite bus driver was in dire straits now gave Aidan an idea. "Why don't you come here for the summer? You're always saying you want to see our country, now's the perfect time. You can stay at my place. You would only have to pay your way over and back."

Larry liked the idea but had always felt uncomfortable staying in people's houses when he traveled. He much rather preferred hotels, even small inexpensive ones. A whole summer of hotels, though, would cost more than he felt he should spend at this time. Still, staying in Aidan's house all summer didn't feel right. "I don't know, Aidan. I mean, I have no problem with the cost of flying over, but I'd be putting you out a lot, free room and board and all. That doesn't seem fair to you."

"No problem! Between my house and Niall's, I'm sure we can find plenty of work to make you feel like you're earning your keep!"

"You make it sound so tempting," Larry admitted. "I really would like to see your country someday. I've said that plenty of times, haven't I?"

"You have indeed. You should accept my offer before I come to my senses and change my mind!"

The rest of the day Aidan's offer hung on the back of Larry's mind. It whispered to him while he searched various websites for charter tour jobs. It nagged at him as he repaired the leaking kitchen faucet in his apartment. It screamed to him above the thoughts of his ex-wife and kids as he tried to settle in for another dull evening in front of the tv.

It kept him awake all night.

Mack spent days sorting through the backlog of videos he'd been sent over the past several months, searching for a singer to fill Michael's spot. He narrowed the list to a dozen potential singers, then researched each one on the internet and social media. He was looking for more than talent. Attitude was important, as was reputation. Looks played a part as well; anyone would be naïve to think they didn't. Above all, though, he looked for passion. Did a candidate burn inside to sing, to create and share music with the world at large? Would the person being considered for the job want to perform so badly they could think of nothing else, would give their whole heart for a chance to chase after their dreams?

Three singers rose to the top of the list, Colin, James, and Nick. Colin came from Galway and was singing at a pub there on the upcoming weekend. Nick lived in Clifden in the Connemara region and had a gig the night after Colin. James was from Tory Island, a small island off the Donegal coast. Mack wasn't sure when he could see James, but if the other two didn't pan out he'd find a way to hear James perform.

Before he could recommend any one of them to the band, Mack needed to meet with each of the three. "I can catch Colin and Nick on the same trip," he told Kate, showing her their locations on the map. "I'll have to stay over both places, leaving this Friday and coming home Sunday. Why don't you come with me?"

"I wish I could. Patrick and Moira are taking Eamon and Eileen to a doctor appointment on Friday; I promised them I'd be here with Conor and Caitlyn while they're gone."

"Alright."

Mack looked more disappointed than Kate remembered seeing him in a long time. "You've never asked me to come along on your business trips before," she remarked, hoping to draw out whatever was bothering him, sure it was something deeper than her inability to join him. "Why did you want me along now?"

Mack confessed, "I just thought I'd like a second opinion on these musicians."

Kate studied the man before her. "Mack, you've never been one to doubt yourself. Why are you doing so now?"

Feeling the full weight of responsibility for Macready's Bridge's future, Mack admitted, "The whole band could fall apart if I make a wrong choice."

"Bands come and go. It's the nature of the business you're all in. But you already know that. If the band falls apart, it won't be due to anything you've done or haven't done. It's just life." Kate gave Mack's arm a reassuring squeeze. "Your judgment is as sharp as ever. Any decision you make will be the right one."

Buoyed by Kate's words and her confidence in him, Mack set out on his quest.

Colin's show Friday night proved he could sing any style of music, from ballads to pub and rebel songs.

"You handle yourself well on stage," Mack told him after.

"Thanks. I'm glad you liked the show."

"As I mentioned when I spoke to you on the phone, Macready's Bridge is looking for a new singer."

Colin's eyes lit up with the thought his dream of singing as a full-time career could come true if the band hired him. "I'd love to be considered for that spot. I'm a huge fan of theirs; I'd love to join them on their tour this year."

Mack leveled with him, "I'm afraid there won't be much of a tour. With Michael leaving and the band in transition, we won't be going to America this year." The fact that major festivals had failed to sign the band was better left unsaid.

The twenty six year old singer's eyes clouded over as he watched another dream disintegrate before it even had a chance to take shape. "That's too bad."

Mack read Colin well, and knew what the singer's decision would be even as he asked, "Are you still interested in the job?"

"Can I think on it a day or two?"

"Of course." Mack rose and shook Colin's hand, sure he'd seen the last of the lad.

The venue Nick appeared at in Clifden was smaller than Colin's in Galway; Mack found the more intimate setting a perfect backdrop for Nick's smooth, rich voice and engaging personality.

Joining Mack at his back corner table after the show, Nick waved the waitress over. "Whiskey, double," he ordered, "no ice." He then turned to Mack. "I hope you found the show worth coming out for."

"You sing very well." Mack watched Nick's eyes dart from Mack to the waitress and bar tender, then back to Mack. "I know you have another set coming up in a few minutes. I'll make it quick. I mentioned to you the band I manage, Macready's Bridge, is looking for a new singer. Would you be interested?"

"Would I ever!" Nick, at thirty-two, had waited years for a crack at the big time. "With me at the helm, Macready's Bridge will shoot through the roof!"

At the helm? Mack watched Nick take a long swallow of the whiskey the waitress had delivered. For all the talent Nick possessed, Mack found an arrogance in him that just didn't sit well. "Nick, you realize the band has been together for years, and they make decisions as a team, there isn't one person alone at the helm."

"Oh sure, that's how they've worked in the past." Nick drained the glass before him and motioned to the waitress for a refill. "I won't steamroll them," he added, sensing Mack's concern. "I'll listen to what the boys have to say before I make any decisions for us all."

"That's fine." Mack checked the time. Nick's second set was due to start. "I best let you get on with your work. I'll give you a call."

Mack couldn't get away from Nick fast enough!

Back at his hotel room, before retiring for the night, Mack checked his mobile phone for a message from Kate. He not only found that but was surprised to see a voicemail message from James, the Tory Island singer he'd hoped to connect with next.

"Mr. Macready, I just booked a gig in Donegal Town tomorrow night, filling in for a friend of mine who's ill. I thought if you were free you might meet me there. Call me any time, if you'd like, and I can give you details."

Before responding to James, he called Kate. "Colin and Nick were both disappointments. I heard from James though. If you don't mind, I'd like to head to Donegal Town to see him tomorrow. I would be away one more night."

"Of course I don't mind." Kate was relieved to hear an upbeat tone in Mack's voice. "I hope everything goes well."

"So do I; otherwise, I'll have to start over." The sound of Kate's voice coming through the phone made Mack feel very much alone. "Tell me how you are, how your day went. Tell me everything, then I won't miss you so much."

"Everything?" Kate laughed, the sound of her laughter so light and airy it reminded Mack of a songbird singing away near their patio, a sound he always enjoyed. "Let's see, this morning I got up, brushed my teeth, washed my face, brushed my hair."

"Not that much detail!" Mack laughed along with her. "You can skip the mundane moments."

"Alright. The twins got through their appointments okay, the doctor's a bit concerned that the hole in Eamon's heart isn't closing as fast as he hoped, but no cause for alarm yet. Eileen's hearing isn't much improved, the doctor is recommending hearing aids for her. Aside from that they're fine. I stopped into my old dress shop yesterday; Deirdre is doing a wonderful job with it …".

Mack listened until he could no longer keep his eyes open. He bade Kate a good night and fell asleep with her face lingering on his mind.

James McClenaghan performed a set of traditional and contemporary songs, exhibiting a vocal range more extensive than Colin's, and a stage presence that was more self-assured than the almost forceful attention Nick drew.

"I'm glad you gave me a head's up about tonight's show," Mack greeted James after his set was over. "You've really got some talent there."

"Do you think so?" Eagerness for affirmation shone across James's face.

"I do indeed. The information you sent me said you've been singing professionally five or six years?"

"Professionally, five years." James expanded on his background, "As an amateur, on karaoke or open mic nights, another seven."

"And you live on Tory Island? That's quite a remote place, isn't it?" Mack had never been to the island, but knew it was a small piece of real estate off the Donegal coast only accessible by boat.

"It is, so." James agreed. "That means only people who really want to be there live on the island."

"How do you make a living when you're not singing?"

"I've been learning the electrician trade from my father. It's a good career path for the future, but not what I really want."

"You know a career in music is a hard road. It takes all the dedication you've got, and most times you don't reach the top, you won't pull in vast sums of money or gain the notoriety you hope for." Mack held nothing back. "You may never reach the stars you dream of."

James nodded, affirming what he'd heard a dozen times before, what he knew in his heart was the truth. "Aye, I'm well aware it's a pipe dream. I can't think of doing anything else, though. I don't want to wake up twenty years from now and regret that I didn't give my dream a try."

A chill ran up Mack's spine. There it was! That's what he'd been looking for in the person who replaced Michael. The passion, the drive, the will to give everything to the craft of music. James had just what Macready's Bridge needed to fill Michael's shoes. All he'd need now was for James to meet Aidan, Patrick, and Niall, and confirm that there was good chemistry between them all.

"The band I manage, Macready's Bridge, needs a new singer. Would you be willing to meet with them one day next week?"

James's brown eyes gleamed with excitement. "I'd love that! Thank you."

"Alright. Let me check with them all, see what date works best. I'll be in touch."

Larry sat with his coffee, his third cup of the morning, staring at the walls in his apartment living room, contemplating how he would handle the next few months. He'd spent days scouting openings for drivers for other tours only to find, as he'd feared, that the most desirable positions had already been filled and the only openings remaining were bottom of the barrel types he'd just as soon pass on. Even the freight pulling jobs he found were cross country back breakers, and not at all what he would enjoy.

Still adjusting to divorce and the absence of his family, Larry felt the walls of his apartment close in on him, felt the suffocating emptiness inside and around him, and knew he could not survive a whole summer unemployed and unoccupied.

He thought once more of Aidan's offer for him to visit for the summer. The pictures Aidan and the rest of the band painted of their homeland, and the real photos they had shared with him as he'd driven them around America on previous tours, were far more enticing than the flat white walls that surrounded him now. He could use a new adventure, he admitted to himself. Before he lost his nerve, he grabbed his phone and called Aidan.

"Did you really mean it when you offered for me to come visit?"

"Of course!" For the first time since Fionna's news and Michael's departure, Aidan felt excitement for the months ahead. "I've got all kinds of room. We'll have a grand time."

"Won't your girl mind?" Larry couldn't remember her name, just the photo Aidan had shown him once of a girl with gorgeous copper hair and vivid green eyes.

"She'll be away at an art program this summer. Even if she was here, she wouldn't mind."

"Okay then, I'll book my flight and let you know when to expect me!"

Pauline felt her stomach churn at the smell of the lamb stew her mother was preparing for dinner; she rushed to the bathroom, reaching it just before she threw up.

"I should have told you sooner, I have to work an extra shift tonight," she lied to her mother before mealtime, planning in her mind to hop in her car and drive to town, or to the coast, or anywhere for a few hours to make her lie plausible.

She could see in her mother's eyes that her mother suspected something. She would not be able to keep her secret much longer. She hurried out of the house before her mother could ask any questions.

Pauline drove to the top of the hill around the bend from Niall's house, where the scenery surrounding her usually calmed and cleared her mind. Today its medicine didn't work. She felt trapped by the secret she'd carried the last several weeks. If she told Niall, he might break up with her. Either way, the truth would come out soon enough. A few days ago, she'd been strong and brave enough to want that conversation, to take that risk. Now she'd lost her nerve, she was terrified, but she had no option. She whispered a prayer, picked up her phone, and rang him.

"Hey, love, I was going to call you tonight. How are you?"

"Not bad. How are things on the farm?"

"Much better. We've got the outbreak behind us."

"That's very good." Pauline closed her eyes, took a deep breath, then told Niall, "I need to see you."

"Sure, why don't you come over now? You can have dinner with us."

"I need to talk with you before dinner."

"What's wrong?" Niall had never heard Pauline sound so serious. "Something's bothering you. What is it?"

"Can you meet me up at our hill? I'll tell you then."

Niall's car threw stones into the air as he rushed up the hill that overlooked his farm and the valley behind it, dread filling him as he drove. He was sure Pauline wasn't breaking up with him, yet he couldn't imagine what would be so serious that she needed to speak with him right away.

Pauline was already at the hill. Instead of rushing to meet him, she stood by her car, waiting for him, more serious than he'd ever seen her. He felt his heart drop to his feet.

"What's wrong, love?" He asked.

Pauline had rehearsed a dozen ways to deliver her news. Now that the moment was here, all her preparations flew out of her mind. Instead, she blurted out, "You love me, don't you?"

"Of course. You know I do." Niall's heart crashed inside him. "Hey, I know I was kind of cold to you the last time you stopped by, and I haven't given you much attention the past couple of weeks, what with Michael leaving and the band struggling a bit, and then the sheep crisis; but yes, I do love you. Nothing's changing that."

"Nothing?" She couldn't stop the tears from flooding her eyes and spilling down her cheeks. "Niall, I'm pregnant."

Of all the scenarios that had raced through his mind since Pauline's phone call, this had not been one of them. Unprepared for her news, he was at a loss for words.

Pauline mistook his frozen silence for denial that he'd had any part in her predicament. "Before you even ask, you are the father."

"It never crossed my mind that I wouldn't be!" Niall fumbled through his shocked mind for the right words to say. "What do you want to do?"

"Do?" Pauline was incredulous. "I'm keeping it, of course.

I don't know what to do. My parents are going to hit the roof! I don't know how I'm going to handle them. You know how strict they are. They didn't talk to my sister for almost a year after she moved to America. They were dead set against her going out on her own. They only softened their heart at Christmas. They didn't even want me working at the pub, except we needed the money. They'll flat out disown me when they find out what I've done!"

Niall's mind raced. In the space of a few short weeks, he'd lost the tour he'd planned on, was in danger of losing his band, had pulled the farm through a serious risk to their sheep, and now this. Overwhelmed, he couldn't think fast enough.

Pauline, impatient and needing quick direction, snapped, "Don't you have anything to say? Forget it! Forget I even told you! We're through!"

She wheeled around to get back in her car. Niall grabbed her arm to stop her. "Hold on! Give me a minute to think, will you?"

"Think? What is there to think on? I'm pregnant! You're the father! If you don't want to step in and help, I'll figure it out on my own! I'll join my sister in America and figure it out from there!"

"Who said I didn't want to help?" Niall realized he was shouting and lowered his voice. "You've had time to adjust to this. It's all new to me. I just need a minute to think."

Pauline shook her head, fresh tears falling down her face. "If you love me, the answer should be clear."

"There's only one answer. We'll get married."

Pauline protested, "You sound like you're trapped. I won't get married like that."

"What the hell do you want from me, then?" Niall exploded. "You're carrying our baby. I'll marry you, take care of you both."

Pauline had dreamed over the past year how Niall would propose to her, if he ever did. She'd dreamed of marrying him and building a life with him, on his farm or wherever else he wanted to live. His offer now fell so far short of what she'd dreamed she couldn't bear the letdown. "I want you to marry me because you love me, not because you have no other choice."

Niall would have laughed if the situation hadn't been so serious. "Ye daft woman! Of course I love you! I would have gotten around to asking you even without this. I was just waiting until my life was a little more settled. I love you and I want to spend my life with you, with or without a baby on the way." He drew Pauline close to him and hugged her.

Pauline let the warmth and security of Niall's arms around her seep into her body and convince her everything would work out right. "Oh Niall, I love you too. I didn't want things to go this way, but we can make this work, can't we?"

"We can indeed," Niall promised her. "Let's not say anything to anyone just yet. Let's figure out when and where we want to get married. You can move into my house until we have time to sort out whether we want to stay there or find our own home. Once we have all our ducks in a row, we can show your parents and mine that we're responsible, that we have this all well thought out, not let them think this wasn't planned. Are you okay with that?"

"I am. We can't wait too long, though. I'll start showing soon enough and then we'll be in a right mess if we haven't told them beforehand."

5

Aidan played for a third time a recording of an early Irish harp song he had come across during his hours of internet research. As he listened to the rise and fall of notes, his mind converted them from harp to guitar and opened in his mind a vast ranging vista of where he could take the music.

"What do you think?" He asked Niall when the tune was done.

"I like it. I don't recognize the tune; has anyone covered this before?"

"I don't think so."

"What's your idea with it?"

"I thought we could change the tempo, either bump it up a bit, or bring it down a notch, like this." Aidan lifted a guitar from its stand and toyed with two versions of the tune they'd heard, one version faster and the other slower.

As he listened, Niall imagined where he could fit his uilleann pipes into the song. Not the whistles, he thought. The pipes would fit better. "I like both versions. Run through the last one again."

While Aidan played the slower version on guitar, Niall pulled out the uilleann pipes he'd brought over with him and intertwined accompanying notes around the ones Aidan played.

"Patrick should have no trouble sliding his fiddle in on

this." Niall set his pipes aside. "Great job finding this one."

"Thanks. By the way, I talked with Larry the other day. You know, our bus driver in America. I've invited him to come here for the summer; he hasn't found a job yet to replace the tour we canceled."

"I never thought how canceling our tour would impact him. Having Larry visit here is a good idea."

"I think it would be fun for both Larry and me, take our minds off an otherwise boring long stretch of time."

Niall watched as Aidan gathered the plates and glasses from their pizza and pints. He so badly wanted to tell Aidan his predicament; yet now that a perfect opportunity had opened, he didn't know how to begin. He didn't know why he was so nervous. Of all the friends in his life, Aidan was the least judgmental. At last Niall said, "I have some news as well."

"Let's have it," Aidan set dishes in the sink and continued cleaning, expecting Niall to say something along the lines of "we're getting a new car", or "another one of our ewes has had her lamb". He froze when Niall announced, "Pauline's pregnant."

The last thing he expected Niall to say, Aidan stopped cleaning and stared at him.

"What are you going to do?"

"We'll get married, of course. Then I think we'll be moving in with my parents, at least for a while."

"Have you set a date yet? Do your families know?"

"We haven't told anyone yet, well, except for you now."

"It sounds like you've got your plans all figured out. What are you waiting for?"

Niall pictured Pauline standing in front of him, eyes filled with tears, jaw set with pride and determination. He knew whatever dreams she'd had for her life had now been altered forever. "I'd marry her tomorrow," he confessed to Aidan, "but she's lost enough of her dreams. I want her to have a proper wedding, church, dress, party, the whole thing. That might take a couple of months to plan and carry out."

Aidan was about to caution him to not take too long in planning, a warning he was sure Niall didn't need, but his phone interrupted. Mack's name and number flashed across his phone screen; he answered the call.

"Mack, Niall's here, do you want this on speaker?"

"Yes." He waited until they both could hear then informed them, "Aidan, I know you were looking forward to having us come out to your place so you and Niall could meet James and for you all to start working together, but Patrick's two youngest have come down with fevers. He doesn't think he should leave them. Would you mind both coming up this way instead?"

Niall agreed right away, but Aidan hesitated.

"Aidan?" Mack called out, "Is that okay?"

"Sure."

Mack could hear the disappointment in Aidan's voice. "I'm sorry. I know you were looking forward to us being there."

"It's not that," Aidan started, then stopped. Anything he might say would pale in importance compared to two sick kids. "It doesn't matter. We'll both be there tomorrow."

"What were you going to say?" Niall asked after they'd ended the call.

"Nothing." Aidan couldn't let it go at that, though, not after drawing truth out of Niall the way he had. "It's just, Fionna's leaving for New York in a week, she'll be gone all summer, and I was looking forward to being here with her, even though I'd be busy with you and the band most of the time."

"I'm sorry, Aidan. It seems both of our plans are turned inside out."

Aidan glanced at his friend once more. Whatever disappointment he felt was a drop in the ocean compared to Niall's problem. "I'll be fine," he told Niall. "Fionna and I have plenty of time ahead of us. As for you, I know Pauline being pregnant changes how you might have done things up, but does it matter in the end? All the fancy wedding bit, that's all just trappings layered over what really matters. You said yourself the two of you would marry anyway. No matter how you set it up, you and Pauline will be fine when all's said and done."

When Aidan told Fionna that evening about the change of plans, instead of being upset as he thought she would be, she took it in stride. "Aidan, I'll be packing and getting artwork and supplies ready for my trip. We'd both be tied up with what we must do, you wouldn't be missing that much time with me."

Aidan knew he should have been grateful that Fionna accepted the change of plans with such grace. Still, a part of his heart was disappointed. Did his time with her mean so little to Fionna that she could let it go with such ease?

He brushed negative thoughts away. Fionna was right. They would not have much quality time while the band was busy practicing and she was sorting things out for her summer away.

Relieved that she wasn't upset, he promised Fionna, "I'll make it up to you. This weekend, when I get back and before you leave, I'll take you someplace special for dinner."

As he and Niall traveled to Mack's house, Aidan thought about the personalities that made up Macready's Bridge and how a new person taking over Michael's place would fit in. He knew band members often changed, people came and went for various reasons, nothing was permanent. He also knew the balance of personalities in any close-working unit was fragile; any shift in that balance threatened to break that delicate bond.

As the only parent of the group, Patrick was the one they all counted on to be steady and dependable. He was the band's rock, the easiest going, the most relaxed, and in both rehearsals and shows the most agreeable to anything that came the band's way.

Niall was simple, straightforward. Aidan suspected Niall had inherited that trait from his parents, and was no doubt shaped by their sheep farm environment where so much was basic and direct. Niall could be counted on, when working with the band, to speak out if a song or arrangement didn't feel right, and to maintain peace between them all when rare disagreements erupted.

Aidan knew he was more complex than Patrick or Niall. His quiet moods ran deeper than Niall's peaceful ones; and where Patrick would stop practices midstream to point out a passage in a song where he thought they weren't in sync, including the group as a whole in his comments, Aidan would single one or another of them out for singing a wrong note or playing with faulty timing. He often held his feelings inside until they built up; then, like a boiling kettle releasing steam, all his feelings would tumble out in a swift stream.

Michael had been complex as well, more moody than even Aidan, although his charismatic nature and humor had smoothed over any rough edges.

How, Aidan wondered as he and Niall turned into Mack's driveway, would James fit in with this mix?

Aidan had his answer soon enough. After running through several Macready's Bridge songs, to which James held his own although singing them in his style, not the same way Michael had sung them, Patrick, Niall, and Aidan each found James to be a talented singer with an easygoing charm.

They practiced well into the afternoon, enjoying the sun

62

and rare lack of breeze on Mack's patio, choosing songs that James was most familiar with. As Mack oversaw their work he noticed, although they were amicable with each other, the spark, the magic that had existed between Michael, Aidan, Patrick, and Niall was missing with James. He hoped in time the magic would return.

They had almost finished a lengthy afternoon practice session when Caitlin ran out to the patio, interrupting their practice with, "Dad, Mum needs you right away!"

Fearing another health crisis with one of their children, Patrick hurried upstairs to the bedroom the two younger twins shared, and found Moira with Eamon on her lap, rubbing his back with brisk circular strokes, panic written across her face.

"He's not breathing well, Patrick! I'm scared!"

Patrick held his arms out and took the boy from Moira. He forced his voice to remain calm. "Let's see here. You're feeling poorly, are you now, Eamon?"

The boy nodded; Patrick noted his flushed face and glassy eyes. "Moira, call his doctor and ask whether we should take him in, or if they can prescribe something for us. Isn't this the same as what he had a couple of months back?"

"I think it is, Patrick. Respiratory distress, I think they called it. I still have the inhaler they gave us for him last time."

As Moira called the doctor, Patrick worked at coaxing Eamon to breathe in the medicine the inhaler contained, while Caitlin and Conor stood against the wall in the younger twins' bedroom, worried eyes fixed on Patrick and Eamon.

"Will he be okay Dad?" Caitlin asked, her voice just above a whisper.

"He will be!" Conor insisted, then turned to Patrick, seeking affirmation. "Right Dad?"

"He will indeed, Conor. Eamon's been through this before and he's come through each time, hasn't he now?"

Conor and Caitlin both nodded, desperate to believe their father.

"Alright then, let's all trust he'll be fine this time as well. Now, why don't you both say a wee prayer for your brother, then run down and see if you can help Uncle Mack and Aunt Kate with dinner."

Moira returned moments later, a slight look of relief on her face. "The doctor thinks it's another respiratory infection. We're to pick up a new medicine at the chemist's; if we don't see improvement in forty-eight hours, we're to take him into the clinic."

"Shall I run out then, while you stay here with the kiddies?"

"Thanks Patrick, but do you mind if I go with Kate instead? I've a few other things I want to pick up as well."

"And you could do with a bit of fresh air." Patrick read the exhaustion across Moira's face, knew she was close to tears with the worries she'd bottled up inside her the past day or two, and a trip out, even as simple as to the local shops, would do her a world of good. "Go on, then. I'll manage things here until you get back."

Thankful that Eileen was still napping, unfazed by the turmoil the last hour had brought, Patrick settled into the rocking chair with Eamon on his lap, rubbing his back in circular motions until Eamon's breathing relaxed and the boy nodded off to sleep.

By morning Eileen was fully recovered, chatting away at the breakfast table to anyone who would listen, while Eamon, breathing much easier than the previous day, was content to sit on his mother's lap. After a casual breakfast, the band moved to the living room as a soft rain prohibited them from practicing out on the patio.

After running through a half dozen songs, Aidan called

for a break. Turning to Mack, Aidan stated, "I think we've practiced as much as we can for a start. You brought us all together so we could meet James and discuss whether he's a good fit for the band. I think we can have that conversation now."

Mack agreed. "James, why don't you step outside for a few minutes?"

"There's no need." Patrick motioned for James to sit back down. "James gets my vote to join us if he'd like."

Niall agreed. "I think you're a good fit, James."

Aidan didn't give an immediate yes. Instead, he asked James, "You're from Tory Island?"

"That's right."

"I've never been there. What is it like?"

"Small." Images ran through James's mind as he tried to describe his home island. Short and narrow, the remote island, accessible by boat or ferry from Donegal, contained only a handful of houses and commercial buildings. "It's a tight knit community there. Everyone knows everyone," James answered, then added, "everyone knows everything about you."

Aidan picked up on the tone underneath James's words. "Are you a singer because you're passionate about music? Or is it a means to get you off the island?"

Caught off guard, James turned the question over in his mind before responding, "Both, I guess."

"That's an honest answer." Aidan nodded at James, and told Mack, "I think you should sign the lad up!"

"Patrick has his hands full these days, hasn't he?" Niall observed as he and Aidan headed home. "Maybe it's a good thing our summer tour was canceled."

"I'm not sure I'd go that far," Aidan countered. "You're right about his hands full, though, especially with Eamon."

"Aye, he does indeed." Niall grew quiet, turning a dozen thoughts over in his mind until his worries overwhelmed him. "Do you suppose children are always such a bother?"

"Don't do that!" Aidan could tell where Niall's thoughts were leading him. "You and Pauline will have no problems raising a houseful of children. Sure, you'll run into hard times here and there, but you're going to find your way through them all just fine."

"I hope you're right. Hey, how about you and Fionna and Pauline and myself going out for dinner before she goes off to New York?"

"Sure. I want to take her out for a special dinner, but I'm sure we can fit something else in before she leaves."

When Aidan stepped into his house, though, he found all his plans had changed. Fionna had brought two suitcases down to the living room and was upstairs in their bedroom filling a third small case with makeup, skin lotions and hair care products.

"What are you doing? Aren't you going to need these the rest of the week?"

Fionna's face, when she turned to him, was a mixture of excitement and panic. "Oh Aidan, I'm glad you're home in time! They've called me to New York early, I leave tomorrow morning."

"But I thought . . .". Aidan cut his protest short. What was the sense? Fionna couldn't help having to leave early. It was out of her hands. His dinner plans destroyed, he returned downstairs, poured himself a tall stout, and left Fionna to finish her packing.

6

Fionna departed the plane and wound her way through Customs, her stomach turning somersaults the size of Atlantic Ocean waves in a torrential storm. Excitement and fear battled each other for control over her movements as she proceeded to the baggage claim area to collect her luggage. As she stepped out of the baggage claim area to meet the Gatewood representative she was assured would be there, she reminded herself of the dozens of times over the past few years she'd had to push past her fears to reach a goal. Each time before when she'd forced herself to overcome a fear, the end result had been rewarding. This was another of those times; she convinced herself the outcome would outweigh the fears that threatened to paralyze her.

Ed Kimbrough met Fionna by the exit door. "Thank you for coming in early. As I mentioned in my phone call the other day, one of our art academy contacts is hosting a cocktail party tonight, we have the opportunity for a few of our most promising students from our summer session to attend, and we'd like you to be one of those students."

The words "most promising" hung in Fionna's mind as Mr. Kimbrough hailed a taxi and they merged into the flow of traffic exiting the airport roadways.

Watching New York City scenes on television and cinema was nothing like being part of the real experience. Fionna tried to take it all in at once, fascination with the scenery as they drove towards the city and with the people hurrying down sidewalks towards various destinations, while at the same time keeping a nervous eye on the taxi as their driver maneuvered it through and around traffic. Once a car almost hit the taxi, once a bicyclist appeared out of nowhere swerving to avoid the cab as if it were nothing more than a tree root in the bike's way, yet their driver appeared unfazed, taking such incidents in stride as if they were normal occurrences.

The cab pulled up in front of a brick building. "Our students are housed in several apartment buildings near the academy," Mr. Kimbrough informed Fionna. "You'll be in this building. The academy is around the corner. I'll show you your place here, then let you get settled. I'll come by later today to show you the academy and then escort you and two of our other students to the party tonight."

Fionna's apartment was on the top floor, a one-bedroom unit with a small bathroom and combined kitchen/sitting room space. In one corner of the apartment, Fionna found the boxes of art brushes, sketching pads, canvases, pencils, and paints she'd sent over ahead of her. Thankful she didn't know anyone here and would not be entertaining, Fionna decided the sitting room would be the best location to set up her easel and art projects for the duration of the summer program. The room had a large picture window with a view of the streets below and buildings nearby; its northern light exposure would be perfect for painting and drawing.

By the time Ed Kimbrough returned, Fionna had unpacked her clothes, sorted through the art supplies she'd had delivered, and dressed for the party, wearing loose black slacks, a flowing black top, a turquoise beaded necklace and earrings, all of which set off her copper hair which she'd fastened back with a turquoise and copper barrette.

Ed Kimbrough nodded approval when he came to collect Fionna. "You look all set for a party! Come with me, I'll show you the academy, and we'll meet the others who will be joining us."

Fionna was pleased to see the academy was a shorter walk from her apartment than she had guessed from the map she'd been sent. Set in a tan stone building, the first floor contained a reception desk, an office, vending machines for beverages and snacks, and off to the right a sizable room where the works of past and present students were displayed.

On the second floor six instruction rooms were set up, divided by movable walls for occasional times when larger rooms were needed. On the top floor, a more formal room had been set up for special exhibit events.

The limousine Ed had booked appeared to take them to the cocktail party. As they were driven across town, Fionna met the other two students, Elizabeth, from Connecticut, and Joseph, from Tennessee. They each seemed as nervous and excited as she was, keeping conversation to a minimum, wondering what they were about to be thrust into.

Having experienced cocktail parties in Dublin, Fionna knew she was expected to circulate, network and connect with guests so they would, with any luck, remember her name and follow, perhaps even buy, her artwork. Ed Kimbrough introduced her to the first few guests, then she was on her own.

The trick, she had learned over time, was to keep conversations short, light, mention her name and her connection with whatever sponsor was hosting the event, answer any questions a guest might have, then move on.

As she worked her way through the room, Fionna noticed

a man standing off to the side whose eyes were fixed on her. At first, she took it as a compliment, a confirmation that she'd chosen the right outfit and looked as radiant as she pretended to feel, instead of the mass of nerves that churned inside her. His gaze remained locked on her as she met with several guests; the longer he remained zeroed in on her, the more uncomfortable she felt. When she at last stepped away from a woman who had held her in conversation several minutes with multiple questions about Ireland, she determined she would approach this man, find out who he was and, if she felt he posed any risk, bring it up to Ed Kimbrough.

The man had disappeared. Fionna scanned the room searching him out, but he had vanished and did not reappear the rest of the evening.

Macready's Bridge moved to Aidan's place for a week of more intense practice. They started their third day with the same positive mindset as they had the previous two, trying to familiarize James with their renditions of traditional tunes before guiding him through their original songs. They started the morning with Foggy Dew, a song every Irish singer knew. Macready's Bridge's version of the song slowed and rearranged the tempo and tweaked the musical phrasing in places where they believed different accenting would lend more power to the lyrics, changes that had been Michael's suggestions which his replacement, James, struggled to adapt to. After two hours of missed cues and dropped accents, Patrick rolled his eyes, Niall exhaled an audible sigh, and both looked to Aidan to take charge of the situation.

Still not sure, after so many years, how he'd been appointed unofficial leader of the group, Aidan shrugged at Patrick and Niall, then turned to James.

"I know every singer has his own style," Aidan started out, choosing his words with care, not wanting to crush the lad's spirit. "I know our versions of songs you've grown up singing might be a little different, but you do have to try a little harder to capture the way we're doing them."

Aidan could see James's jawline tighten and his body go stiff. "I'm doing the best I can. It's early days. I'll get them in time."

"I'm sure you will. Mack's in there on the phone trying to book some gigs for us, though, and we're nowhere near ready for them yet. Do you think you could try a wee bit harder?"

James flashed angry eyes at Aidan. "I thought Mack was the manager here. If he has a problem with my singing, I'm sure he'll let me know. Why don't you just let him do his job and stay out of it?"

"That's not how we handle issues among us," Patrick told James, quick to diffuse tensions before they flared out of control. "We try to work things out among ourselves, rather than leaving it all for Mack to sort out."

Aidan stepped in. "Don't take what I said out of context. I'm not saying you're a bad singer, I've told you before you're up to the job. I'm just saying we have a lot of work to do before we're ready for any of the gigs Mack lines up for us. We need you to focus more."

James glanced from Aidan to Patrick to Niall who, although silent, showed from the look on his face he agreed with Aidan. In a flash, two choices rose to mind: he could quit now, let the other three perform their songs however they wanted, he would find another job, or he could continue to pour everything in him into learning the songs with the exact nuances Macready's Bridge had written into them, proving to the other three he could do it.

He considered Macready's Bridge's past success, how in just a few short years they had reached the top of the Irish music world. Even though their standing had slipped a bit, he had no doubt they would reclaim their top spot soon enough. He wanted to be with them when they did.

James promised Aidan and the rest of the band, "I'll work harder at learning the songs."

As the band rehearsed, Mack tried to book venues for them. Larger venues and festivals had already set their summer lineups; they had no openings for Macready's Bridge. Mack reached out to all the contacts he'd gathered over the years, leaving voicemails for some, sending emails to those he couldn't reach by phone. The contacts who returned messages had little to offer, other than assurances they would keep Macready's Bridge in mind if they had any cancellations.

Only one pub owner, Owen Kavanagh, came right to the point. "Is it true Michael Sullivan's left the band then?"

"He has," Mack confirmed. "He's always wanted a solo career, and he had an offer he couldn't refuse."

"From Diarmid Fitzsimmons, right?"

"Correct." Mack felt the same stab of pain he experienced every time the name of the man who had drawn Michael away was mentioned.

"Mack, I'll be up front with you. Not many are willing to take a chance on a reconstructed Macready's Bridge until they've proven themselves. Get a few covers out, give everyone a chance to hear how the new singer fits in, and the bookings will come."

Mack knew Owen was right. Macready's Bridge was still in early days of restarting. God willing, better days were ahead of them. For now, all he managed to book was a dozen gigs spread throughout the country.

That evening, Mack handed each of the boys a sheet of paper listing the dates, times, and locations of bookings he'd been able to make. "Alright boys, here's a schedule of upcoming gigs for you. It's just a start. I have messages out to a number of additional contacts; I'll update each of you when I book any more shows."

James took the paper without comment, not grasping how bare the schedule looked.

Niall and Aidan exchanged glances, telegraphing to each other in silence their dismay at the lack of bookings. "Is this it?" Aidan asked, stunned.

Mack sank into an empty chair across from him. "We're starting fresh, Aidan. A lot of places are already booked for the next few months. Other places want to see how James fits in." Mack looked at each of the faces focused on him. "I know it's not many shows, and it won't generate much of an income for you. It's going to be a hard few months. I have faith in each of you, though. Macready's Bridge will come back, I'm sure of that. We just need to get through this next while."

Moira reviewed the schedule Patrick texted her as she settled in for bed. "It's not that bad," she told him when he called a short time later, relieved to see the amount of time he'd be away was minimal. "This leaves you more time with us."

Patrick reacted as if she'd announced the end of football season would be a good thing. "You're joking! Did you read the damn thing?"

"Of course I did! I still don't see what you're so upset about. It's not like Mack hasn't booked anything at all for you."

"Are ye daft? We'll be losing money on this! These pubs will be paying to scale. Anything we pull in will just barely cover our travel expenses! What do ye think we'll be living off of the next few months? Mack and Kate's good graces?"

The toll of another long day of chasing after and worrying over her children swept over Moira, and she allowed her concerns to spill out. "I'll be honest, Patrick. I'm glad you're not touring America this summer. I'm glad your schedule is light. I need your help around here. Eamon and Eileen are more of a handful than Conor and Caitlyn ever were."

"I thought Kate helped you out a lot. She did last year while we were touring, didn't she?"

"She did, and she still does."

"You do know bookings and tours are what the band's goal is, right? At some point we're going to be away, maybe for a month or so at a time, like we have before."

Tears rose in Moira's eyes. "I know. But I need you here, Patrick. I need your help."

"You're confusing me, Moira. Kate's very helpful, but you told me while we were on holiday you want to move back to our house near Sligo. You understand my job, but you want me to stay home."

"I know I'm confusing you. I don't even know what I want anymore." Overwhelmed by the constant stress she was under, feeling weak as the day drew to a close and all her inner turmoil spilled out, she leveled with Patrick in a way she hadn't for a long time. "The past few years have been so hard. You haven't always been home to see it. All the fear surrounding the twins' premature births, yes, we were thrilled they were born, but it's been a roller coaster emotional ride ever since. Eamon's heart condition. Eileen's hearing. All the worry I carry inside me. I don't let on to you, or even that often to Kate. I'm trying my best to handle it all. Every day they make me laugh and fill my heart with so much love, but at the same time I'm so afraid of what their future will be, if they'll run into health problems I won't know how to handle, of whether I'll be able to look after them and safeguard them as much as I want to. I know I'm all over the place, Patrick. I can't help it."

A wave of guilt washed over Patrick as he began to understand the fullness of Moira's worries. "Shhh, love, don't cry. It's alright. I'll be home for a while; we know that much. You know there are support groups for parents of twins and preemie babies. If you want, we can look into them. Outside of that, I don't have any answers for you right now, but you're not alone in this, we'll get it all sorted as time goes by."

Moira considered what she knew she and Patrick had in their bank account. "I know our money's going to be tight for a while."

"It's not just the money," Patrick explained as he stretched out on the bed in one of Aidan's spare rooms, tired after another long day of practice and the various frustrations both the band and his wife had presented him. "We're used to having more requests for bookings than we could accommodate. This just feels such a letdown."

Moira commiserated with him, "I know. I know there are new acts on the scene replacing Macready's Bridge's standings on the charts. Festival and show promoters have snatched them up, leaving little or no room for you and your band. I understand Michael's leaving has hurt you all as well. I also know you all have the talent and drive to overcome this. You'll reclaim your spot in due time. I have faith in you."

Patrick didn't share Moira's confidence in what the future would hold for him and his band.

In their individual rooms, separated by a short distance between them, each feeling alone, Moira and Patrick turned lights out and settled down for sleep, trying to believe each others' words of assurance would prove true, fearing the unknowns and the myriad things that could go wrong.

Settled in her apartment, prepared for her first round of classes the next day, Fionna brewed a cup of tea, wishing she'd thought to pack some good, strong, Irish tea instead of having to suffer the weaker American beverage. With her unpacking finished and apartment organized, she settled on the sofa and tried to calm her nerves over what classes would be like. Starting work with new instructors was always an ordeal until she grew accustomed to their methods of critiquing.

With little else to crowd her mind, thoughts of Aidan flooded in.

Even though he hadn't said so, Fionna knew Aidan had been upset when she'd had to leave for New York earlier than planned. In her excitement she'd brushed aside thoughts of him, but now Aidan was all she could think of.

Sometimes, in reaching for dreams, one had to give up some of what one loved in life, if only for a while. Aidan knew that. He'd been through that enough in pursuit of his musical dreams, even leaving Fionna behind the last couple of summers while he was on tour.

This time it was her turn to leave him behind. It would only be for the summer, she reminded herself; she'd be so busy she'd have little time to miss him, and surely he would be busy enough himself he'd have little time to think of her.

With the prospect of classes ahead of her and sleep closing in, Fionna finished her tea and headed for bed, reminding herself over and over, like one counting sheep, that she would rejoin Aidan soon enough.

7

James gazed out the kitchen window of his father's cottage to the hills of Donegal, separated from his Tory Island home by the Atlantic Ocean, now roiling from increasing winds signaling an incoming storm. Just home from his first full week of practice with Macready's Bridge, his mind was less on the day's work ahead with his father, and more on Aidan's warning to perfect his handling of the band's songs. Fear that he would not fit in with the group after all magnified in his mind until, like the ocean, his mind, heart, and nerves churned in mixed directions, confusing the course he had fixed his vision on. Perhaps, after all, he was wrong to think he could build a career in singing.

"Will ye be giving me a hand with work today?" his father called to James from outside, interrupting his thoughts.

Running electric through a new house on the west side opposite where he and his father lived was the last thing James wanted to do. He would much rather stare out at the sea and dream his dreams of success, or replay Aidan's words over and over and nurse his wounds. When the Old Man called, though, there was no disobeying. "Be right there, Da," he called back, drank the remains of his morning tea, and grabbed his jacket.

Paul McClenaghan thrust a tool belt towards James. "Your mind's been a million miles off since the ferry brought you home yesterday. What's that about?"

"Just thinking over rehearsals." James placed the tool belt and his and his father's lunch boxes in the back of his father's truck, then slid onto the passenger seat as his father started the engine.

"And how did rehearsals go? You've hardly said two words about your time away."

"Fine," James started to say, then stopped himself. "Truth be told, Da, I didn't get on well. They've got tricky arrangements to their songs. I don't quite have them down yet."

Mr. McClenaghan steered his truck along roads until they arrived at the new building site. The framework of a two-bedroom cottage stood waiting for the insertion of wires, outlets and switches that would send a pulse running through the house once connected. "That band you're joining didn't rise to the top with sloppy work. They've set high standards for themselves. If ye want to be playing along with them, you best be raising your own standards and work your tail off for them."

"I will," James vowed, bristling at his father's harsh tone. "They could go a little easier on me, though. It's only been a couple of weeks since I was hired. It takes more time than that to perfect the tunes the way they've got them arranged."

More concerned with the amount of work to be accomplished that day, Mr. McClenaghan told his son, "Ye know what I think? You're too soft inside, too easily wounded. This band meant nothing in coming down hard on you, I'm sure, but that ye need to step up your learning of the songs. If you want that dream bad enough, ye best toughen yourself up inside and get the job done."

With that, Mr. McClenaghan turned his back to his son and focused on the work at hand.

As he worked in unison with his father, James considered

with a fresh view the island he'd spent his life on. A small strip of land, rock hard base with shores shaped and reshaped as wind and sea wore at its edges, Tory Island was separated from the mainland by Atlantic waters smooth one minute and turbulent the next. Only a few hundred men and women with great inner strength and fortitude could withstand its isolation. Most of Tory's inhabitants were artists, story tellers, and musicians dedicated to maintaining as many of the traditional ways of their heritage as they could.

In that, James fit in with those around him. He was born with music flowing through his blood and had started singing as soon as he could talk. Unlike his fellow island inhabitants, though, James held no desire to remain on this narrow strip of land. He still remembered how his mother, stricken with a gastric ailment in the midst of a very bad winter storm, could not be transported to Donegal to receive advanced medical help in time to save her. Eleven at the time of her passing, James had vowed he would find a way off Tory and build a better life for himself.

Music was his only hope of fulfilling that vow. Too soft inside? On the contrary! He'd show his father he could be as tough as the Old Man himself! He'd learn those songs better than the band themselves knew them! He'd fight his way to the top if he had to, and leave his father and Tory Island far behind.

Larry stared out the airplane window to the land and sea below him, still finding it hard to believe he was about to arrive in the country he'd heard so much about.

Once he'd made the decision to take Aidan up on his offer to spend the summer at Aidan's house, he'd been filled with a deeper excitement than he'd known in the past three or four years. The past few years of driving tour buses to and from Irish festivals across America, widening his exposure to Irish musicians, their music, and their culture, had fueled his desire to someday visit this intriguing land. As he packed, he'd imagined all the adventures ahead, castles and landmarks to visit, pubs to become familiar with, and most of all time spent with Aidan, Niall and Patrick. Of all the musicians he'd escorted across America, the Macready's Bridge lads had been his favorites, always courteous, always having fun, rarely a cross word or bad incident between them. Even though Michael had left the band, Larry hoped he would see him somewhere along the way. Whatever the summer had in store for him, Larry knew it would be a trip he'd never forget.

Now, as his plane approached Dublin, in the morning light he could see patchwork fields through clouds, a blue ocean marked by whitecaps, and the most dramatic coastline he'd ever imagined.

"Welcome to Ireland!" Aidan greeted Larry as he cleared Customs and the baggage claim area at the airport. "I'm so glad you could make the trip over. I promise we'll give you a good summer here."

"I know you will. Thanks for letting me stay with you."

Aidan laughed. "I didn't have to twist your arm very hard! You were looking to escape for a bit, even if you didn't realize it."

"I was, and your offer was a true godsend."

"I hope you don't mind us not spending time in Dublin now," Aidan apologized as he stored Larry's suitcases in the back seat of his car and drove them away from the city. "I thought you'd enjoy it better when we can spend a few days there, do the city up proper."

"That's fine. Whatever works best with your schedule is fine with me. There's so much I want to see here."

As Aidan maneuvered his car across motorways and narrower roads to his house, Larry took in the countryside they traveled through, moving swiftly out of the Dublin region past the same patchwork fields he had seen from the air, past fields lined with golden gorse, through villages so small one road defined them, and larger ones with neat shops and pubs, a thatched roof here and there, and streets so narrow two cars passing almost touched.

Mesmerized by all that he saw, Larry at times didn't know which way to turn his head for fear of missing something. "All the pictures you've shown me don't do Ireland justice!" Larry spotted a round castle standing in the middle of a town they were passing through. "Hey, can we check that out?"

"I'll add that to our list. We're almost at my house now; I'm guessing you could do with a bit of a rest before dinner, then we'll start making a list of all the places you want to see."

Aidan parked his car in his driveway and shut the engine off. "Here we are then," he announced to his passenger. "What do you think?"

Larry stepped out and surveyed the house before him. "Good Lord, Aidan! You said your house was big, but I didn't expect this. This is a mansion!"

Aidan recalled once again the turn of events in his life that had prompted his move from Derry to this country house. "The size was a bit daunting when I first looked at it," he admitted now, pushing painful memories down deep inside his heart, "but there's great potential for building a future here. That's what I needed, a change, something to look forward with, to not be bogged down by the past. Plus, Niall and his family are right across the way, there, and that made the move easier. You'll meet them all later today; we'll be joining them for dinner. Come inside, and I'll show you around."

Aidan led Larry through the living room, dining room, kitchen, and upstairs bedrooms, ending in the rear bedroom at the other end of the hall from Aidan's. "This is your room if it's okay with you. You can take any of the guest rooms you'd like, but this one has its own private bathroom right off it, and you have the best view of my property behind the house."

Larry surveyed the scene out his window. "What a stunning view! Is that smaller building your new studio?"

"It is. I'll show you that now; then you can catch a little rest if you want before we go to Niall's place."

Larry followed Aidan back outside and across a short stretch of land, marveling at the panoramic scene that spread out from them on all sides, the rise and fall of hills, the expanse of blue sky overhead unbroken by city skyscrapers or billboards, how the sky was mirrored in the lough between Aidan's and Niall's houses, and how quiet the space around him was compared to the apartment he'd left behind. No rush of cars or trucks broke the silence, no sirens, no shouts of neighbors, no radios or televisions blaring. The silence felt foreign to him, although not in an uncomfortable way. Larry found himself so taken in by his surroundings he almost forgot to follow Aidan to the studio's entrance.

"Aidan, this is amazing!" Larry took in the control board, microphones, lighting, oriental rugs, and chairs set around the old carriage house. "You're really setting yourself up for a successful business here."

"It's just a start." Aidan glanced around the room, pride swelling inside him as he took in the various pieces of equipment and furniture he had gathered to date. "Someday I hope this will be a prominent recording studio. For now, it's a good place for us to rehearse and record Macready's Bridge material."

"How is the band doing?" Larry thought again of how Macready's Bridge's fortune had slipped over the past several months, and how Michael's departure had added to their struggle to rise back up in industry standings. "How is Michael? Have you talked to him since he left the band?"

"I've had a couple of short chats with him, the last time a week or so ago. He says everything's going well." Aidan recalled Michael's words from their last conversation, less for their content than for the underlying tone behind them, as if Michael had hoped to convince Aidan working with Diarmid was smooth sailing when in fact it was not.

Larry picked up on Aidan's hesitancy. "You don't believe him, do you?"

Aidan shook his head. "No, I don't know why but I have a feeling it's not all sunshine and roses for him. I could be wrong." He paused, then added, "I hope I am."

Michael opened a new water bottle and drank from it, glad for a break in the long morning of recording he'd already put in, with so much more to come. As the water cooled his tired throat, he tried to calm his mind.

You knew it would be like this, he reminded himself. Diarmid told you you'd be covering other people's works, that he planned to give you more of a supporting role at first to get people to know you, before launching a solo album for you.

I know, his alter ego argued back. I just didn't think supporting role meant burying me so deep in the background my voice could barely be heard.

He'd been stunned at the playback he and the other singers had just listened to. Even though he knew right where his vocals came in, what parts were his, the places where his voice rose and then faded out, listening to the recording they'd just made he found his voice buried, overshadowed by Bridget O'Leary, the lead soloist, and Tricia and Robbie, the other two background vocalists hired for Bridget's album.

Michael knew he needed to discuss his feelings with Diarmid. It wouldn't be easy; Diarmid was known for having a fixed vision that no one could persuade him to change. He made quick decisions then stuck by them straight through to the end of a project. Still, Michael had to let his frustrations be known. Diarmid had gone off for a meeting while Michael and the others were to continue recording that afternoon. He was expected back around dinnertime.

Catching time with Diarmid was harder than Michael thought it would be. After Diarmid returned to the studio he was caught up in phone calls, then people streaming in and out of his office with various questions and needs. Michael waited over half an hour, at one point almost ready to give up. He knew he had to resolve his concerns, though, and remained in the office reception area until his turn came.

Diarmid rose, shook Michael's hand, and motioned to a chair across the desk from his own, waiting for Michael to be seated before settling back into his own leather chair.

"What can I do for you?"

All afternoon Michael had rehearsed in his mind what he wanted to say. Now, seated across from Diarmid, his well-planned dialogue vanished. He had no choice but to plunge right in and not waste his manager's time.

"I was surprised when we listened to this morning's playbacks. I know I'm a backup singer on this project, but I could hardly hear my voice at all."

Diarmid had been down this road with other performers under his management. He knew just how to appease them.

"Remember I told you we were going to start you out

gradually, feature you on albums with artists already on our label who have strong fan bases, build you up from there."

"I remember," Michael agreed, "but I thought I'd have a bit more of a prominent role on other artists' albums. I feel like I'm buried behind the other background voices."

With the patience of a father explaining a basic principle to a toddler, Diarmid told Michael, "You feel invisible because you're used to having your vocals stand out. The songs you recorded today were just a beginning." He reached into a desk drawer, withdrew sheet music for two other songs, and slid them across the polished mahogany desk surface. "I wasn't going to give you these yet, but I've been considering these songs for duets between you and Bridget."

Michael ran his eyes over the sheet music. Both songs looked to be the kind of romantic ballads he'd had his sights set on. He would have preferred to someday have these songs appear on his own solo album; but if singing them duet fashion with Bridget would provide him more exposure, he was fine with that.

"I'd love to do these as duets," he told Diarmid.

Diarmid gathered the sheet music back. "Fine. Let me get extra copies of these. I'll discuss them more with you and Bridget next week."

Michael had warned Susannah he'd be late coming home for dinner. He arrived even later than he'd expected, to find Susannah waiting with wine and glasses at the ready, and chicken marsala warming on the stove.

"How did your talk with Diarmid go?"

"Better than I hoped." Michael kissed Susannah, opened the wine, and poured a glass for each of them. "He showed me music for a couple of duets he wants me to sing with Bridget."

"That sounds promising, doesn't it?"

Even though Susannah tried to sound positive, Michael caught an edge in her voice. "You don't sound too thrilled."

Susannah set her wine glass down and turned to face him straight on. "If the duets work out, I'll be very happy for you. Over the past few weeks, though, I've watched you go from excitement over Diarmid's initial offer to disappointment and this afternoon to outright anger. You're excited again and that makes me happy. I just hope Diarmid keeps his word and things work out the way you want."

She didn't say what was foremost on her mind. Since they'd married, she had been waiting for Michael's career to stabilize to the point where she and Michael could start raising a family. She'd seen and heard of so many former friends of hers who were living in houses now and having children, it had started preying on her mind. She'd suppressed her yearnings long enough; inside her heart, her desire for a child fairly screamed at her at times.

She couldn't say any of that to Michael, though. He was under enough pressure. Instead, she finished her wine, served their dinner, then chose a historical program on the television, the kind Michael liked the most, and nestled next to him on the sofa.

Michael focused half his attention on the program Susannah had chosen. The other half of him was centered on Susannah. While there was truth to her words, he was sure something else bothered her, although he couldn't quite name it. She'd been more moody than usual over the past couple of weeks. The two or three times he'd pressed her on it, she'd passed it off as concerns about her work and refused to say any more, snapping at him if he asked too many questions. He was sure something besides either of their jobs preyed on her mind; he would just have to wait until she was ready to let him know more.

James stepped outside the ceilidh he'd been enjoying and inhaled deep breaths of clean night air. While the air inside was warm, and the chill night air had already started to penetrate his jacket, he still preferred outside.

He'd always loved the ceilidhs Tory Island was noted for. On an island as small as Tory, every inhabitant knew everyone else, and the ceilidhs were like large family gatherings. The music and stories shared were always great craic, fun, and the pints and food always prime. Tonight, though, James found the food, the people, and the music all dull.

He studied the stars overhead, crisp and bright against their dark navy backdrop, and imagined the darkness was a blackout curtain spread across the sky, and the stars actually sunlight poking through holes in the dark curtain. The sound of waves breaking in rapid succession against the rocky cliff edges not far from the ceilidh house had a steadying, anchoring effect on him, sweeping away the claustrophobic, suffocating feeling that had overwhelmed him inside.

He tried to figure out why, when he'd been to so very many similar events over the years, he felt so different tonight. It took a while, but he eventually figured it out.

He was bored.

The traditional music he'd listened to all his life, and sung time and again over the past several years, failed to inspire him tonight. No matter how much he loved singing, he was tired of songs he'd sung a hundred times over. He wanted, no needed, something fresh. He felt the same way about Tory Island. While he loved the traditional way of life the island's inhabitants had devoted themselves to, and the centuries old customs he'd grown up with, he craved change. One small island seemed much too limited for him when beyond the island's borders, on the other side of the water that held that island apart from the mainland and the rest of the world like a microcosm encapsulated in its own solitary cocoon, the life he yearned for screamed his name.

James remembered, as he watched the stars overhead twinkle their own Morse code pattern he wished he could decipher, how he'd learned singing from his uncles and neighbors, eventually joining them at ceilidhs and smaller gatherings. It had seemed enough for him until, on a trip to the mainland with his father a dozen years earlier, he'd seen a video of a popular music band playing to an enthusiastic crowd. In an instant he was star struck, and knew performing was what he wanted to do for a living. Remaining on Tory would not provide the opportunities or exposure he would need to reach the heights of success he dreamed of.

He'd hoped the gig with Macready's Bridge would be his ticket out; thinking back now, he was less confident. No matter how hard he'd tried, and he had put as much effort as he could into it, he couldn't quite get the unique beat and timing Macready's Bridge had used to transform traditional tunes almost everyone in Ireland knew into new, fresh arrangements. He'd returned home from the week of rehearsals feeling he'd let Mack and the band down.

Now, with the stars and waves standing guard over him and the rest of Tory's inhabitants, as they had for millennia, as he listened to the music and laughter carrying on inside the ceilidh house without him, as he thought of his father, already asleep at home, preparing his body for another day of the constant physical demands of wiring new buildings, James knew he stood at a crossroads. Either he pushed harder for his dream of a different life, committed everything inside him to reaching his goals and finding his way off this tiny island, or he'd give music up altogether and join his father in the electrician trade.

He made his choice even before he'd finished forming the words in his mind.

8

Niall had just finished clearing the kitchen from the noonday meal he'd shared with his parents before they headed to Omagh for their monthly meeting with friends, Will with fellow sheep farmers to discuss the latest news and trends, and Anna to meet the other farmers' wives for tea and cards, when pounding on the farmhouse's side door so loud it startled him broke the house's peace. Even as he rushed to the door to see who was there, the pounding grew louder and more urgent. He opened the door to find Pauline, crying and panicked.

"They know," she cried out. "My father's furious! He's kicked me out of the house."

"Come in! Tell me what happened. How did they find out?"

"I'm showing, Niall. Look at me." She stepped back and ran a hand over her belly, now protruding the slightest bit through her jeans. "My parents aren't stupid. They confronted me, and I couldn't lie. They knew before I said a word."

"Did you tell them we're getting married? That we're sorting our plans out and then we'll be married?"

"My father doesn't want to hear that. He doesn't want to hear anything! He told me I let him down, I broke his rules and the rules of the church. He told me to get out!"

"What about your mother? Didn't she stand up for you, take your side at all?"

"She's caught in the middle. My father's always shown you

his good side, but make no mistake, it's his way or no way at all in our house. Why do you think my sister moved to Chicago? She couldn't wait to get out of our house and away from our father!"

Niall thought back to his visits to the O'Shea household. While it was true that Helen, Pauline's mother, was the warmer of Pauline's parents whenever he came for tea or to pick Pauline up, her father, Daniel, had always shown him respect and had neither displayed anger nor coldness towards him. Pauline had hinted a few times that her father was strict, but Niall had never pushed for details, and she had never offered any.

Pauline was devastated now, though; that much was clear. Niall felt compelled to try to sort things out with her father.

"Let's go back to your house. If your father sees we're intent on building a life together, and that this baby is very much wanted and will be well cared for, maybe he'll soften his stand."

Niall turned to fetch his car keys, but Pauline grabbed his arm and forced him to stop. "You're the last person on the face of the earth he wants to see right now. Just leave him be."

Niall stared hard at her, trying to decide the right course of action. "Alright," he relented at last. "I'll let him go for now. Do you need to go back for clothes or anything else?"

"No, I have a suitcase in my car with whatever I could grab fast. That's all I'll need for now."

Niall pulled a kitchen chair out for Pauline. "Here, sit down. I'll get your suitcase, then I'll make us some tea and we'll work things all out."

The New York City Fionna entered was nothing like the Dublin, Ireland she'd left behind, or the New York City she'd anticipated. Where Dublin had been familiar, small and manageable, and the New York City she'd imagined had been tinged with the soft edges that always accompany dreams, the city she encountered was large, noisy, with the soft edges of her dreams replaced by cold, hard cement and indifferent, preoccupied people. Fionna found herself alternately intimidated by and enthralled with her new surroundings. The city held so many neighborhoods, each one different with its own style and flavor; she didn't know where to start in her explorations and found herself afraid to venture very far on her own.

Entering her first class session, Fionna was surprised to see the man who had been so focused on her at the cocktail party standing at the front of the room welcoming them all in.

"Fionna, our lovely Irish lass," he greeted as she stepped into the room.

The only one called out by name as they all took their places at tables and chairs, Fionna felt a mixture of flattery and embarrassment. She caught how he held his eyes upon her a few seconds longer than his visual pass over the other students.

"I'm not going to pair you up for assignments," Dennis Ryder, their instructor, announced to the class of eight students. "You're in a strange city and I know pairing you up would give you security, but I want each of you to form your own impressions and generate your own ideas for the assignments I give you, rather than relying on feedback from each other.

"For your first assignment, I want you to explore the city, and create a piece of artwork that captures some sense of your hometown or region."

Throughout their first session Fionna had noticed how charming Dennis was, the depth of his brown eyes, how his dark brown, shoulder length hair curled the slightest bit behind his left ear, the stubble of dark beard visible despite the early hour of day, the dimples that peeked out whenever he offered the class a smile. Thoughts of Dennis followed her outside the classroom, intruding on her concentration over her first assignment until she pushed him out of her mind.

With three days to complete her assignment, Fionna first thought of the many Irish pubs scattered across the city, the piped Irish music they played during the week, and the live weekend music as various bands performed songs she'd grown up with. The three pubs she visited each gave her the feeling of home, with music that stirred her heart as it always did. Entering the pubs alone, though, caused her to miss friends, and Aidan in particular, far too much. What would she paint of these pubs, she wondered. The large hole they drilled into her heart?

Fionna toured the Irish Tenement Museum but found the depictions of cramped living quarters and desperate conditions too heartbreaking as she listened once again to stories of hardship and poverty faced by her Irish countrymen moving, penniless, to a country that did not always welcome them with open arms.

She found the inspiration she sought at Ellis Island, not in the long rows of empty benches, or the suitcases stacked along a wall, or the antiseptic medical rooms through which so many immigrants had to be examined before being granted entry into America, but in its stories of hope, and a window which offered an immigrant's first view of the Statue of Liberty.

Unsure which medium would best capture the scene, Fionna tried two approaches, first using charcoal pencils in a black and white study of the image, then with oil paints capturing the white exterior edges, the black inner framing effect and, in the small center opening, the famed statue itself, Lady Liberty offering hope to so many dreamers who desired to enter America's shores.

"I like that you presented two different takes on this view," Dennis started their private evaluation session with, examining the charcoal and oil pieces Fionna presented. "That's a very original take on an iconic image. What made you choose this?"

Fionna recalled the powerful impact of her few hours at Ellis Island. "I wasn't going to go with such an obvious image, and the long history of Irish immigration to America, but I saw this view through one of the windows at Ellis and it attached itself to my heart with such force that I had to go with it in the end."

Dennis found Fionna's passion as she spoke captivating. She was his sixth evaluation session of the morning; her enthusiasm was refreshing after so many students who answered his questions with caution, afraid to make a bad impression on their instructor. "Tell me why you chose both the charcoal and oil mediums."

Fionna looked again at her artwork, recalling the feelings each one brought out in her as she worked. "Charcoal is very light, delicate to work with, as you know. In a short period of time, I could capture the image in my mind and gain more immediate gratification than working with oils presents. The charcoal drawing isn't as heavy as the oil painting, it's more one dimensional, but I like its relative simplicity. On the other hand, with oil paints I could layer colors as the photo it's based on layers emotions, I could draw the viewer in, create the dark framing that the real scene presented, and of course the colors of water and Lady Liberty are much more appealing than the black and white charcoal image. I couldn't make up my mind which one to show you, so I brought both."

Dennis scrutinized the pieces once again. "You have a nice light touch with the charcoal, you could go a little heavier with your brushstrokes in oils. Overall, your technique is very good."

After all eight evaluations were finished Dennis announced, "You've each done very well your first week. For your next assignment, I want you to spend some time at the Metropolitan Museum of Art. Study the difference in brushstrokes of various paintings there. Don't focus on light and dark, or composition or viewpoint. Focus on the brushstrokes. See what they tell you."

"Sleep well?" Aidan teased as he handed Larry's first cup of coffee over to him. The clock showed nearly half ten, Aidan had already washed a load of laundry and hung jeans and shirts on the outside line to dry, reviewed and paid the latest round of bills, and replied to a dozen emails.

Larry accepted the coffee, closed his eyes, and inhaled the dark brew's strong aroma. "Why did you let me sleep so late? You should have got me up earlier."

"You looked tired yesterday, I decided to let you sleep in." Aidan laughed as he added, "Don't expect that treatment every day!"

"I was tired," Larry admitted, although he knew that wasn't the only reason he'd fallen into such a deep sleep.

The apartment he'd moved into after his divorce had never felt like home, it was merely a place to shelter his belongings, to take his meals and pass his time in between jobs. Its walls, devoid of pictures and other decorations which he'd not yet found the desire to hang, felt cold and sterile. No amount of television or music could cover the pervasive, suffocating silence.

Here at Aidan's house, Larry already felt more relaxed, felt his bones ease and his muscles loosen their tension. It might have been the size of the house, with its spacious rooms that still retained a warm coziness despite their size; or perhaps it was the wide open vista the large windows in Aidan's house offered, providing views of fields edged in the distance by trees and hedgerows, and unbroken sky. Aidan's presence in the house helped as well. Knowing he was not alone removed an invisible pressure his shoulders had carried; intermittent sounds of footsteps in the halls and stairs, doors opening and closing upstairs and down, and voices from Aidan's radio downstairs drifted up to Larry's bedroom, confirming another human being shared this space, he was no longer isolated. Twice Larry woke up to find dawn or morning light filling his room, twice he thought he should rise and join Aidan downstairs; each time his body drifted back to sleep, ignorant of what his mind dictated.

"I haven't slept this well for months. I haven't gotten used to being alone."

Aidan understood what Larry meant. Before Fionna had moved in, Aidan had suffered several bouts of insomnia, nights when he'd thrown the towel in at two or three in the morning, trudged downstairs, and either picked up one of his guitars and played for a while or stretched out on the sofa with the television on, hoping some mindless program would lull him back to sleep.

"That's why I urged you to come out for a visit," Aidan confided. "I could tell you were struggling with the adjustment."

"You're a good friend. Thank you again for the invite. Now that I'm up, what have you got in mind for the day?"

"We've a fair bit of sunshine forecast." Aidan glanced out the window to confirm what he already knew. "I thought

I'd take you to one of our touristy places, Giant's Causeway, Dunluce Castle, Mussenden Temple. Take your pick."

Larry browsed through the brochures Aidan set before him. Each of the attractions looked intriguing. After several minutes he slid one across the table back to Aidan. "I've heard so much about Giant's Causeway, let's go there."

Aidan called Niall before they left. "Want to join us?"

"Thanks, no. I have too much to do. Are you and Larry joining us for dinner?"

"Sure, we should be back by then."

Aidan drove Larry along narrow roads, some edged by gold blooming gorse, some by fuchsia hedges ten or twenty feet high. Where the visibility was unimpeded by hedges, Larry looked out on wide open fields, some with sheep grazing on them. Occasional cottages dotted the fields, they drove through a few small towns, no more than a few streets wide, before they reached the car park where they would catch the bus to the Causeway.

"Giant's Causeway was formed by molten volcanic lava about sixty million years ago," Aidan informed Larry as he led the way along the path that took them to the field of basalt columns the Causeway was known for. "That's the scientific explanation. We Irish prefer the legend.

"Finn McCool was a giant of Irish descent who was at war with a Scottish giant Benandonner. Finn considered Benandonner to be a threat to Ireland. Finn had a bridge built over the waters that separated the two countries so he could cross over and put Benandonner in his place. He taunted Benandonner to come over and fight him. However, as Benandonner reached the Irish shore Finn realized his enemy was much larger than himself. Finn's wife saw Benandonner draw close, and quickly disguised Finn as a baby. When

Benandonner reached the Irish side of the bridge, he saw the baby, figured the father must be an even bigger giant, and fled back to Scotland. The bridge between the two countries was destroyed, never to be built again."

"I like that version better than the scientific one." They had reached the main basalt column field now. Larry surveyed the hexagonal columns spread out before him and turned to Aidan. "I never imagined anything this incredible."

They walked the length of the region, stepping with care over uneven edges, climbing the mound of columns that protruded out into the ocean. At the highest peak, they stood and took photos of each other, Larry entreating a passerby to take a photo of them both together.

Then they separated and gave each other space for their own reflections.

Larry gazed out over the ocean, wondering if he had ever seen anything so vast and powerful in his life. Waves rushed in, departed, and hurried back, each with the same whisper and the same whitecap spray. He pondered the science and the legend the Causeway site was based upon, intrigued by both, trying to imagine sixty million years ago, or any time when giants and fairies were real. In his mind he pictured two giants sparring with each other, throwing mighty rocks, either to smite one another or, in Finn's case, to break apart an intruder's possible means of access. Many times over Larry had heard what magic Ireland contained, but never thought he'd experience it in person. Now he walked over to an edge where the ocean's waters could wash over his shoes and thought, my God! I'm standing in the Atlantic itself and surrounded by rock formations a giant created!

Aidan tried to not think too hard as he stood atop an array of hexagonal columns. No matter how many times he'd visited here since their passing, memories of his father, sister and grandmother always flooded in like the Atlantic's waters flowing over the rocks upon which he stood. This time, just for this time, he begged God to hold those memories at bay, to not overshadow the happy day he was sharing with his friend.

He tried to block thoughts of Fionna from crowding in as well. Giant's Causeway was a place she loved and had tried several times to paint. Never able to set up her easel due to the winds that blew with such frequency here, she'd taken dozens of photos with varying light, and then tried to recapture the light's magic at home, spending hours with her canvas and paints, never quite able to capture what she'd seen in person.

Balancing himself now on a row of basalt columns, Aidan forced his mind to focus on the present, to look forward, not back. He had music to write and, God willing, if Mack could get the band back on track, to perform. He was excited to have Larry visiting, and to be able to show their bus driver around to places they'd talked about during so many long excursions from one festival to another over the past few summers. He had no time, or desire, for memories or emotions to drag him down.

Standing at the Causeway always inspired him, and Aidan looked for that inspiration now. He considered the volcanic age, eons ago, and how the earth had formed this unique stretch of rock. He allowed himself to be mesmerized once again by the ocean, the endless ebb and flow of waves, the gradient shadings of blue in the waters. He spotted a small wildflower growing out of a crevice between the basalt rocks around him and marveled at the persistence it must have taken for that flower to grow through such a small, hard place. Between the ocean's constancy, the mystery of creation, and the wildflower's determination, the inspiration he sought planted seeds in his mind which he could not wait to translate into music. He showed Larry the various features the Causeway was noted for: the Wishing Chair, the Camel, the Granny, the Pipe Organ and Finn McCool's boot, then hurried them both home, describing his inspirations to Larry as he drove.

By the time Will and Anna returned home, Niall had calmed Pauline down, they'd settled her belongings in a dresser and closet upstairs and charted their course of action.

Will and Anna were not surprised to see Pauline's car in the driveway when they returned home. They were surprised, and worried, to find a very somber Niall and Pauline seated on the sofa, waiting for them.

There was no softening his message, no hinting around, no easing his parents into what he had to say. Niall took Pauline's hand in his and looked directly at his parents. "Pauline and I are going to have a baby. We're going to marry as soon as we can arrange it. Would you mind if she lived with us until we can find a house of our own?"

Always the softer touch, Anna said yes right away. Will, however, always the more cautious of them, had concerns. "Why are you not living at home until you've sorted things?"

Pauline started to give a tearful reply, but Niall stepped in. "Because I've told her she should move in with me. If it's not here, we can find someplace else. We will do, in time, but just don't have that sorted right now."

Will held up both hands. "Alright, don't get defensive, lad. It was only a question." He looked from Niall to Pauline. She was a lovely girl, he thought, in fact he had told Anna that several times. They both thought she was well suited for their Niall. He had thought Niall had planned to marry the girl in a couple more years, when they'd saved enough to secure the home they wanted. Well, that dream was over now. He glanced at Anna, who confirmed his thoughts with an almost imperceptible nod of her head. "Of course, Pauline can stay here. Niall, you know the farm will someday be yours, if you want it. There's no need even looking for another house for you and Pauline, unless you think the four of us under one roof would be a hardship. Your mother and I are both downstairs now. If you and your lovely wee lass here are agreeable, the upstairs is yours."

Pauline looked at Niall. She had often wondered what it would be like to live on the Donoghues' farm. His parents had always been very sweet to her, the serene surroundings soothed her, and she knew if his music business ever failed Niall would be running the sheep farm with his father. Imagining a scenario was one thing, though, and reality often quite different. What if she didn't get on well working in the kitchen with Mrs. Donoghue? What if she someday wanted to paint rooms different colors, or rearrange the furniture or even buy new? What if they had more children and the noise and chaos were more than Niall's parents could handle?

On the other hand, Niall was quite adept at working things out with his parents. Pauline suspected if any problems arose, he could smooth them over.

From her living room position, Pauline could see through a kitchen window to the pastures the Donoghue sheep grazed on, and the silver blue lough that marked the boundary between Niall's and Aidan's properties. The air outside was quiet save for the sounds of an occasional bark from Farley, the Donoghues' dog. Any other place they might find would not be this peaceful or homelike.

Funny how life turns out, Pauline thought. She'd carried so many dreams inside her, of marrying a handsome man, of a grand wedding at one of the castle venues their country was noted for, and settling into a newly built house with all the modern amenities, a far cry from the run-down house she'd grown up in. She had the first of her dreams. Niall was handsome, and more than that he was kind and patient, and a hard worker. The other two dreams, well, her father had often warned her against building castles in the air, hadn't he? If she faced disappointment now, it was no one's fault but her own.

Besides, Niall would be a good husband and father. Will and Anna were pleasant to her, and even if they weren't, what options did she have?

Niall, waiting on her approval, looked so hopeful. All the love she felt for him rose again in her heart. Church weddings, castles and fancy new homes meant so little, she realized. What mattered most were the people that filled this room.

"If your parents will have us," she told Niall, "I think we'd be happy living here."

"How did your visit to the Met go?" Dennis asked Fionna in class a week later. "Which paintings did you choose, and what did you learn about the artists' brushstrokes?"

"I chose *The Penitent Magdalen* by Georges de La Tour, *Old Woman Praying* by Mathias Stom, and *Flowers in a Blue Vase* by Adolphe Monticelli. Georges de La Tour's brushstrokes in *Magdalen* are so smooth they're almost invisible. I like the silky elegance of this painting. Mathias Stom's brushstrokes are more visible, adding depth and realism to the *Old Woman*. Monticelli's brushstrokes in *Blue Vase* are the boldest.

"Why do you think each artist chose the style he did?"

Fionna thought back on each piece. "I know that artists use different strokes to capture or portray certain aspects of light, but I took a different view. Georges de La Tour wanted the subject in his painting to be the focus. He wanted to remain invisible, let the art speak for itself. Stom, I think, wanted some texture in his works, the brushstrokes are part of the story his painting tells."

Dennis nodded approval of her answers. "And Monticelli? Why do you think he used such a bold style?"

Fionna pictured the artwork again. Her least favorite style, she chose him only to complete her assignment. "He wanted to be bold, to be 'in your face' with his painting. He's flaunting his strokes, demanding that you notice them."

"Very good," Dennis agreed, trying to decide whether Fionna's shining copper hair attracted him more or her gleaming green eyes. Or was it the lilt in her voice, her Irish accent so alluring he almost forgot to ask his next question. "Based on what you've seen from those three artists, which style appeals to you most? What would you like your paintings to reflect?"

Fionna knew her answer immediately, but she took extra time in considering each piece in order to not appear too inflexible. "*Magdalen*," she replied. "I want my strokes to be unnoticeable like that."

Dennis observed, "From your portfolio I can tell you've already been focusing on invisible brush strokes. I notice you don't have many portraits in your portfolio. A portrait as exquisite as what you've chosen takes a very delicate, experienced touch. This week I'd like to see you try to copy the *Magdalen*, see how closely you can match de La Tour's techniques. I'd also like to see you imitate Monticelli's harsher strokes in the *Blue Vase*."

Fionna had not anticipated that assignment. Terrified that she would fail, she told her instructor, "Both of those painters are masters. I'm sure it took them years to perfect their techniques. I don't know that I can capture their level of expertise in a few short days."

"Then you best get started today." Dennis noticed the apprehension etched across Fionna's face. "I'm not expecting perfection. Remember, you're here to learn new techniques. I'll be here to help if you have any problems."

9

Mack, Kate, Patrick, and Moira lingered with rare second cups of tea at the breakfast table while the Leahy children were upstairs dressing for the day.

"I better call and make sure Aidan's ready for us to come out to his place for practice tomorrow." Mack picked up his phone and rang through.

"Aidan, are you ready for Patrick, James, and me to spend the week there?"

"I sure am. Larry's here now, you might have to sleep on the sofa. You don't mind, do you?"

Mack missed the teasing note in Aidan's words, his mind zeroing in on how his back would not enjoy nights on the sofa. What was wrong with the lad, he wondered! By now Aidan knew a proper bed was best for his physical comfort and well being. "I'll take the sofa if it's all you've got left . . .".

Aidan laughed, knowing he'd gotten his boss once again. "I was teasing about the sofa; I've plenty of room. I know you're an old man and your bones are falling apart!"

"Cheeky beggar! That's enough out of you!" Mack laughed along with Aidan. "Tell Larry I'm looking forward to seeing him."

"Will do. And you're bringing some of Kate's shortbread with you, right? Don't bother coming at all if you don't have that in hand!"

Mack played along with Aidan. "I don't know that you've earned the shortbread. We'll be over mid-morning."

"Everything's set. Kate, can you whip up a batch of shortbread for me to take tomorrow?"

"For Aidan, of course."

Patrick pulled a long, hurt face. "You never make shortbread when I ask for it!"

Kate teased back, "You don't have Aidan's sweet smile!"

"Shot down again!" Patrick feigned hurt, then rose from the table, motioning for Moira to join him. "We best go see what our young ones are up to. They're a bit too quiet this morning."

Mack helped Kate clear the table. As they worked, he asked her, "Will you and Moira be okay with Patrick and me gone for a week?"

"We have been all these years, we'll manage now." Kate set a stack of dirty plates on the kitchen counter and faced Mack. "I'll miss you, though. I always do, even when it's only a few short days."

"That's not a bad thing," Mack quipped, carrying on the teasing tone of the morning. "You'll appreciate me all the more when I come home!" Then he drew Kate closer to him and gave her one of the most passionate kisses they'd exchanged in months. "There'll be more of that when I return, give you something to look forward to!"

Upstairs, Moira and Patrick found Conor and Caitlyn helping Eamon and Eileen dress and brush their teeth, a task the elder siblings had voluntarily undertaken in recent days. Often amazed at how perceptive her two older twins were in recognizing and taking on some of the challenges their younger brother and sister represented, Moira thanked them now.

"I'll take over from here," she told them. "You two should start in on your schoolwork. Your list of assignments is posted on the school website; I'll be in soon to see how you're getting on."

Moira finished getting Eamon and Eileen ready for the day, then stepped into the bedroom she and Patrick shared. She watched as he packed shirts and jeans into a small suitcase, fighting within herself to find a balance between her anxiety over yet another of his absences and her recognition that the demands of his work made occasional absences necessary.

Moira's audible sigh alerted Patrick to her presence. Bracing himself for another battle over yet another trip of his, he turned to face her.

"Everyone all set for the day?"

Moira nodded. "Conor and Caitlyn are starting their assignments, and Eamon and Eileen are watching their favorite video show."

Watching as Patrick continued to fill his suitcase, Moira voiced the thought that had been uppermost in her mind during breakfast. "I don't understand why you can't continue to practice here, instead of going all the way out to Aidan's place."

"It's less than two hours away, Moira. I'm not jetting off to the other side of the world. Aidan's got better equipment at his studio and, to be honest, fewer distractions."

Moira latched onto his last words. "Is that what we are then? Distractions?"

Patrick threw socks and underwear, meant for his suitcase, onto the bed. "Good God, woman! Will you be twisting around every word I say?"

"You're making it sound as if we're interfering with your work!"

"And you make it seem as if I'm choosing work over family, and you know that's not true!"

"Do I?"

If Moira had slapped him across the face, it would have hurt less. Patrick glared at her. "If you don't know that by now, there's little hope for us."

Both worn out by constant skirmishes over this subject, Patrick and Moira froze at his words.

The fine line between expressing feelings and verbal war was razor thin. Moira knew if she took one more step across that line her words would cut so deep she and Patrick might not recover. She took a step back.

"I get that it's easier to practice at Aidan's, and I know it's not the far ends of the earth. I've tried to tell you how hard it is for me when you're away. Fair or not, that's how I feel these days. When you're on the road doing shows, I understand that. Rehearsals, though, are something else; I just wish that could be done here."

Taking his cue from Moira, Patrick checked his anger as well. "I shouldn't have said distraction. You and our children mean everything to me. If you don't know that, I'm doing a bad job of showing it. I'll only be gone a week. I'll call you every night like I always do; and I'll be home before you even have time to miss me."

"Larry, it's good to see you," Mack greeted the bus driver who had escorted them around America through so many tours. "I'm sorry our plans didn't work out this year; I hope that's not why you were left short of work for the summer."

"It's not the sole reason. In a way it's good things fell apart like they did. Thanks to Aidan here, I can finally see some of the country you all have told me so much about."

"I'm sure Aidan will take you around to some of our best spots in between the practices and gigs we have lined up. What do you think of his place here?"

Larry cast his eyes around the studio they stood in now, and the view of the house across the lawn from them. "He's got some set up. I say give Aidan ten years and he'll have one of the major recording studios in the business."

"Five years," Aidan corrected, coming up behind them with a tray of coffee, tea, and pastries. "You know I put everything in my life on a fast track!"

"I also know if we don't do well this year you may have a lot more time to advance your studio." Mack tried to keep his words light, upbeat, yet he knew the seriousness of their situation weighed them all down, whether they chose to admit it or not. "Everyone grab tea or coffee and a pastry if you want, and let's get started. We've got a fair amount of work ahead of us. James, have you worked on the list of songs I gave you?"

"Aye, Mack." James drew his attention away from Aidan's impressive house and studio and back to his new boss. "I've still a few rough spots to iron out, but I'm getting there."

"Fine. We'll start with those songs."

They worked well into the afternoon going over and over songs Macready's Bridge had recorded before, with James taking on Michael's parts. If Patrick, Niall, or Aidan grew tired of James slipping in the difficult spots time after time, they never let on. They broke for lunch and later for dinner and went to bed late at night satisfied with their progress.

Their second day went better. "You've caught on well," Aidan praised James during their afternoon break.

"I know you all took a chance on me," James answered. "I'm doing my best to not let you down."

"You're doing fine."

"Niall, is that your lovely lass bringing food from across the way for us?"

Niall looked to where Patrick pointed, where Pauline was crossing the field from the Donoghues' house to Aidan's, carrying a large box that looked far too heavy for her. He hurried out to help her.

"I told you I'd come over to fetch all this!"

Pauline only smiled. "I know how hard you've been working. I didn't want you to have to take time away that you didn't need to."

"You shouldn't be carrying anything this heavy by yourself. What have you got in here?"

"Ham and cheese sandwiches, salad, and an apple cake your mother helped me bake."

By now they had reached Aidan's house. They set the box with its goods on the kitchen table, then Niall drew Pauline out to the studio. After introducing her to James and giving the rest of the band a chance to greet her, he pulled her closer to him.

"You should know, Pauline and I will be getting married soon and you're all invited to the wedding. We don't have the details set yet; I'll keep you all posted."

Congratulations circled the room. Grateful no one asked about what led to their sudden announcement or pressed for further details, Niall and Pauline hugged each other, she departed, and the band returned to their work.

Satisfied with their progress, by their last day, with rain and wind shuttering them inside Aidan's living room in front of the fireplace, Patrick brought up the new album idea Aidan had described.

"I've been thinking on this. I have a song that might fit, and a title for the album unless something better comes along."

Aidan explained to James what Patrick was talking about. "You weren't with us a few weeks ago when we discussed a new album. It started with a dream I'd had. In the dream, I saw an ancient clan, secure inside a castle while outside warring clans encircled them. The chieftain, or king, of the clan carried a lot of worries inside him, yet he had to remain calm and keep those around him calm as well. He called on the harpist of the clan to play; that music soothed everyone's spirits. When I woke from the dream, I was reminded all over again that's part of the great importance of music, to soothe the spirits of people who hear us, to give them something positive and pretty to counteract all the chaos and stress in their lives. I was also reminded of the vast library of ancient harp and other early Irish music, so much of it untapped, lying dormant. Only a few artists have dipped into the waters of those ancient tunes. I was thinking maybe we could transform and update some of the ancient songs."

Turning back to Patrick, Aidan asked, "What are your thoughts?"

"My father told me a story when I was young and taught me a song that goes with it. He learned it from his father, who learned it from his; it goes back several generations.

"As it was told to me, back in the day when parties were held in neighbors' houses, and the music was flowing along with the food and drink, when anyone would leave at the end of the night any of the musicians still present would step outside and fill the night air with music until the leaving party was home, or at least out of sight. They called it playing each other home.

"This is the tune my father taught me."

Patrick tucked his fiddle under his chin, checked and

adjusted its tuning, and played a slow tune that held each of the band members and Larry and Mack captivated. As he played, Patrick imagined his father, grandfather, and beyond listening from the spirit world they now inhabited.

"That's beautiful," Niall commented when Patrick had finished.

Mack asked, "Do you know who the original composer was?"

"No, I'm sorry. My father never said."

Aidan, the last to speak, told Patrick, "I love it. If Mack can track and clear any copyrights on it, we should use that song. That title phrase too. You know, there's another side to that title, not just playing music for someone on their way home from a party."

Intrigued, Patrick asked, "What's that?"

"All of the Irish who ever had to leave home to make a living in another land, whenever they would hear Irish music it carried them home in their hearts. That's the power of the music. That's why we, and bands like us, have such a strong following, why Irish festivals and the like in America are so popular. We're connecting people with their roots, in effect playing them home."

The rest of the band digested Aidan's words, allowing the full impact of his comments to seep into them.

"I never thought of it that way." Patrick finally broke the silence. "That's deep."

"I agree." Mack nodded to them all, "There's your next album title and concept."

Kate handed a fresh mug of coffee to Moira and lowered herself onto a patio chair where they both could watch Conor, Caitlin, Eamon, and Eileen as they played on the lawn. While

Patrick and Mack had been rained in at Aidan's, Moira and Kate reveled in the warm sun that graced their yard. "Look at Conor and Caitlin trying to teach the younger ones to fly kites! You should catch a photo of that."

"Already done." Moira raised her phone to show Kate. "I've sent some photos off to Patrick. Shame he couldn't be here to see for himself."

"As much as he loves his job, I'm sure he hates missing out on some of these moments with the kids growing up."

Moira lowered her eyes to focus on the column of steam rising from her mug, as she counted in her mind the number of times she'd spoken to Patrick about missing so much of their children's growing up years. Over the past several months it had become an all too familiar theme from her as an up and down battle raged inside her, torn between the constant pressures of raising four children so much on her own, and wanting to support the man she loved so deeply. Even this morning, Conor had resisted when she'd insisted it was time for him to power up his laptop and start in on his homeschooling assignments, Caitlyn was in tears over some argument she'd had with her best online friend, and all Eamon and Eileen had wanted to do was play instead of getting dressed and having their breakfast. Kate, as always, had been wonderful in her help and support; still, in the back of her mind, all Moira could think of was Patrick having a carefree day, sipping tea in the morning and downing pints at night, and doing what he loved without all the demands and responsibilities that threatened to pull her under.

"I've been horrible to him lately," she confessed to Kate now. "I've been hammering away at how I need him here, need his help with our children, and pulling him in two instead of giving him the freedom, the permission, to follow his heart and his music."

"Years back I had the same battles with Mack," Kate admitted. "I kept at him all the time, not because of children, we didn't have any, but about him always being away." With time Kate's memories of that period in their marriage had softened, but some moments came back to her now creating an ache in her heart, not as sharp as the jagged pain she'd felt back in the day, but still sending a wave of guilt to wash over her. "You know our story. Mack and I split up. Oh, not just because of that, we had a number of issues between us. My nagging at him didn't help, though."

Tears welled up in Moira's eyes. "Oh Kate, I don't want Patrick and me to split up over this."

Placing a reassuring hand on Moira's arm, Kate told her, "I'm sure it won't come to that. You and Patrick can work through this."

Moira returned a small smile. "I hope so."

They settled back in their patio chairs then to watch the children fly their kites. Caitlin and Eileen raised their kite, a bright white and yellow daisy against a green background, in short order, Caitlin holding her little sister steady and the much smaller Eileen clutching the string, while the bright white flower soared against a soft blue sky.

Conor and Eamon, at the other end of the yard, had yet to get their Celtic cross themed kite up in the air. Eamon could not run well, forcing Conor to slow his pace which in turn gave the kite little updraft upon which to launch its flight. Showing great patience with his younger brother, Conor leaned over him, helped him hold the string that tethered the kite to them, and tried to help his brother run fast enough to send their kite soaring.

"Your older children are so good with their brother and sister," Kate observed.

Moira beamed and was about to reply when she heard a shout out, "Mom!" It wasn't a cheer, as in "Mom, look! We got the kite up!" The scream was more panicked and sent a chill through her veins even as she turned to see Eamon lying face down on the ground, Conor looking terrified, and the Celtic cross kite floating far above them all, untethered and free.

Moira and Kate both ran to where the Leahy children had gathered. Moira turned Eamon over, took in how pasty white his face was, how his lips had started to turn from pink to light blue, and shouted to Kate, "Call the paramedics!"

Kate had already placed the call, the ambulance sped up the drive just as Moira had carried Eamon, still unconscious, to the front to meet them. As the ambulance rushed to the hospital, Moira gave the paramedics Eamon's health history, his premature birth and his current cardiac weakness resulting from being born so early.

Kate remained behind to comfort the other three Leahy children and, at Moira's request, to call Patrick.

"I'm sorry to get you away from your work," she started out, forcing herself to steady her voice and not panic him. "Eamon had a wee fall, Moira's on the way to hospital with him now."

"Hospital?" Patrick's voice leapt into full alarm mode. "Is he that bad off?"

"I don't think so. Moira just wanted me to alert you. She'll call you in a bit to update you."

"I'm not waiting! If I leave now, I can be to the hospital in a couple of hours!"

He hung up before Kate had a chance to talk him out of his decision.

"I need to go! Eamon's being taken to hospital; he's had a bad fall."

"Let me drive," Mack ordered. "You're too charged up to drive yourself."

Mack drove as fast as he dared from Aidan's house up towards Derry, then over into Donegal and Letterkenney. Moira called once to update Patrick, informing him Eamon had regained consciousness and the doctors were running tests. After her call, Patrick pressed Mack, "Can't you drive any faster?"

"I'm already past the speed limit," Mack pointed out. "If we get caught speeding that will only set us back longer."

"I should never have gone to Aidan's," Patrick lamented. "Moira begged me to stay, told me she needed me home with our kids. I didn't listen to her."

Mack thought of a dozen ways to respond to Patrick, to reassure him he'd done nothing wrong, he was following his job, Moira had Kate with her. The words all rang hollow in his mind; he was sure they'd sound that way if spoken out loud, so he kept silent, focused on the traffic in front of him and the twists and turns of the road they covered, and let Patrick spew out all his fears and regrets.

Mack dropped Patrick off at the emergency room door, then parked his car.

Eamon beamed as Patrick entered the curtained off area he and Moira had been stationed in. "Daddy! You're here!"

"And where else would I be if you're poorly?" Patrick glanced at Moira, saw the fear deep within her eyes despite her forced smile. Not wanting to push for too many answers in front of the boy, he turned his attention back to Eamon. "What happed to you?"

"I fell flying a kite."

"Did you get it to fly very high?"

"Not too high. Conor helped."

"Alright. Let me talk to your mom and the doctor, then we'll go home."

Outside the curtain partition, Dr. Candler explained, "Eamon's cardiac artery illness caused him to lose consciousness, the same as we've dealt with before. You said he wasn't running very fast when this happened?"

"Not too fast at all," Moira reiterated. "Is Eamon getting worse then?"

Dr. Candler double checked Eamon's chart before answering. "I don't believe so, but I'd like to see him in a month. If he has any more episodes, or anything at all that concerns you, call my office. We may need to adjust Eamon's medicines a bit, but we'll hold off on that for now."

Relieved to see the three of them return to the waiting room, Mack rose to meet them. "Eamon, lad, did you keep an eye on those doctors, make sure they're doing their job the right way?"

"Aye, Uncle Mack, they're doing it right."

Mack knelt by the boy. "How about a ride out to the car?"

Eamon climbed onto his shoulders. "Hurry! Let's beat mom and dad!"

"I don't think today's a good day for a race. I'll bet we can get your dad to sing you a song on the way home though, do you think?"

Kate had dinner ready by the time they arrived, beans on toast for the kids as that was their favorite, and pasta salad with chicken for Patrick, Mack, and Moira. After they ate, Moira turned a movie on for the children to watch while the adults chatted over gingerbread.

"Dr. Candler didn't seem too concerned," she filled Kate in. "It took longer for Eamon to come back around, though, than it has before. I'm worried."

Patrick tried to calm her fears. "If there was cause for concern, they would have admitted Eamon for observation instead of sending him home."

"You weren't here to see what happened!" Moira snapped at him. "I was. I know what I saw, and what I've seen every time he's had an episode. You're not very often here when it happens. You don't know."

Patrick kept his eyes on his coffee mug, twirling it in slow circles in his hands as his mind turned over a nagging thought. "Isn't it odd these things only happen when I'm gone."

"Are you saying it's my fault?"

Kate tried to settle both parents down. "Shhh. You don't want the kids to hear you."

"I'm not saying it's your fault," Patrick corrected, "any more than it's my fault for being away. That's just life. If you want, I'll quit my job and be with you and the kids all the time. Is that what you want me to do?"

Moira didn't answer right away. Of course she didn't want Patrick to quit the band, any more than she wanted Eamon to continue having health problems. She didn't know what she wanted, truth be told. She was tired, emotionally drained from this latest episode, from always handling the crises in the children's lives alone, from always having to be the strong one. She knew it wasn't Patrick's fault his job with the band took him away so much of the time. She just was desperate for a break from the constant worry that permeated her mind and heart, and from trying to hold all their lives together.

She told Patrick, her drained voice small, worn out, "I just want everything to be alright. I want our kids healthy. Thank God Eileen hasn't had any of Eamon's health issues. I don't think I could cope with two sick children."

"You know I'm always here to help," Kate reassured her.

118

Struck by the thinness of Moira's voice, revealing a layer of physical and emotional exhaustion in her he'd never fully understood before, Patrick's heart broke for her. At that moment, he knew what he had to do. "You've been a star," he told Kate. "Moira's right, though. I should be home more; but I can't pull out of the band until we complete the shows Mack has already booked for us."

10

Fionna listened as Dennis critiqued the paintings of other students in the class and hoped he wouldn't judge her work with the same level of criticism he was handing out to the rest of the room. Reminding herself his job was to instruct, to point out what artists were not getting right, what they needed to view differently or improve, she tried to give Dennis the benefit of understanding. Still, his tone seemed harsh, he offered very little positive encouragement to any of them. She studied her paintings with a more judgmental eye as he drew closer. Had she done her best to capture the assignment he'd given? Had she imitated the master painters' styles well enough? Were her brushstrokes as invisible as she could make them in her copies of the *Magdalen* and the *Blue Vase*? Or would Dennis's refined eye catch her mistakes?

"Your composition on each of these is fine," Dennis started out as he reviewed the paintings she'd spread out on her work table. "Your use of light and dark, your depth perspectives, all of these are very well done."

Fionna held her breath, waiting for the downside in his critique.

"Your stroke work still needs some attention." Dennis pointed to the first painting. "You did well in imitating de La Tour's invisibility in his brushstrokes, although there's still a little room for improvement. In your Monticelli imitation, you captured his shading fine, but you need more texture. His brushstrokes are heavy. You still tend to use smooth, even strokes. I'd like to see more contrast between the smooth and the rough in your work."

Fionna stiffened, an involuntary reaction Dennis caught out of the corner of his eye.

"You don't much like rough strokes, do you?"

"No," she had to admit. "I feel like I'm forcing them."

"You understand why artists choose them, don't you? We talked about it in our earlier class."

"Yes. They're trying to capture texture, light and shadow, trying to add another layer of focus to their works, to force viewers to observe more than just the subject of the painting."

"What do you find so objectionable about that?"

"I'm not objecting to it," Fionna defended, then stopped herself. The last thing she wanted was to argue with her instructor. "I don't know. There's a tension in the broader, heavier strokes."

"And you don't like tension?"

She didn't. She'd felt enough of it between her parents and herself to never want any more of it in her life. She tried to not think, now, of all the times they'd communicated their displeasure with her dreams, either by giving her silent treatment or disproving looks she could read from the other side of a room. How many times had her stomach been tied into knots for fear of displeasing them?

"No," Fionna admitted to Dennis, "tension's not one of my favorite emotions."

Dennis gave a light laugh. "Alright. We'll work on it some, but I won't force the issue. I've noticed you don't have any night scenes in your portfolio. For your next assignment, I'd like to see your use of night lighting in your next three works.

Select scenes that appeal to you from our city, but please, no Times Square scenes! That's been overdone."

For two nights Fionna crossed the city by bus considering various sites.

The New York Library was an almost instant choice. Although the globe lights under the arches were lit, the lions who guarded the building looked lonely, as if cement lions could feel. By day they greeted hundreds of people climbing the steps and entering the chambers inside that held shelf after shelf, book after book of history, science, philosophy, literature, volume after volume of knowledge and dreams. Now, at night, people walked or rode by paying no attention at all to the feline sentinels who guarded the treasure house.

To complete the sense of loneliness in her painting, Fionna added a young man, a teenager, at the foot of the stairs, looking up to the closed building, crushed that he could not enter.

Fionna's next painting was of a row of brownstone houses with neatly trimmed, colorful window boxes outside first floor windows, and elegant chandeliers glowing warm amber inside. Underneath the halo of a streetlamp, she painted a young couple walking hand in hand, portraying a scene of contentment that matched the secure comfort of the brownstone house interiors.

For her third night scene, Fionna had thought to paint the Brooklyn Bridge at night, it's lights shining like the diamonds that filled the dreams of those who crossed it into Manhattan by day, or the iconic New York City skyline, until she came across a street musician playing saxophone, eyes closed as if he were one with his music, scant dollar bills and coins tossed into his open instrument case, multi-colored lights from neon signs around him reflecting like jewels off his saxophone's shiny surface. Painting that, she thought of Aidan back home, and realized with a stab of guilt she hadn't called him in almost a week. Fionna checked the time now, ten o'clock at night, calculated it would be three in the morning back home, too late to call now. She made a mental note to call him the next day.

"Larry, it's good to see you again." Anna held out a chair for their guest. "Don't be shy; help yourself to breakfast before the others have it all gone."

Niall feigned a wounded look. "Now Mam, do ye think I'd be that cruel? Of course I'd leave something for our American!" He selected the smallest piece of soda bread, placed it on Larry's plate along with a scant spoon of scrambled eggs and a slice of bacon, and smiled at his mother. "There, see? Larry's all sorted!"

Anna slapped the back of Niall's head. "Don't be so cheeky! Pauline, love, pass that basket of bread to Larry. Larry, get yourself a proper serving of eggs and bacon, and never mind how much you take. We've plenty more."

After all their plates were filled, conversation turned to the task for the morning.

"Larry, are you still up for an introduction to sheep farming?"

"I'm looking forward to it," Larry answered Niall. "Aidan, is there time before we leave for Derry?"

"It depends." Aidan sent Niall a conspiratorial wink. "Niall, will you be showing him the slaughter end of the business?"

Niall played along with the teasing. "I did think to, but if you've plans that can't be shifted I suppose I could put that off for another time."

Will caught the nervous look on Larry's face. "Don't pay them any mind, lad. They're just after teasing you." He gave

Niall's arm a light rap. "Stop mistreating our guest! And you as well, Aidan!"

"Da, he's not a guest, he's more a friend, our bus driver who's seen more teasing from us than you know!" Still, Niall and Aidan pulled back on their fun.

After breakfast, Niall led Larry out to the barn.

"We'll start with our recordkeeping." Niall pulled out a spreadsheet and pointed to various columns. "A sheep farm, like every other business, has to be viable. Here we track every ram, ewe and lamb, how many ewes a ram mates with, how many lambs each ewe produces, whether each ewe has an easy delivery or needs assistance. Once she's had her lamb, or sometimes twin lambs, we track how attentive she is with them, whether she nurtures or neglects them, and how healthy each lamb is."

Larry scanned the various notations on the chart. "I don't have to keep anywhere near as detailed a listing of the vehicles I drive! What are the numbers here on the left?"

"Each sheep has to be tagged with an identification number; they're followed from birth to death." Niall saw the sad shadow that flickered across Larry's face. "We're a small farm. We're growing, mind; I have plans for our future as I'll someday take over here for my father. Small or large, though, no farm can afford to carry animals that aren't earning their keep."

"No, of course you couldn't."

"Let's go outside now." Niall pointed to the pastures closest to the barn and house. "Grazing is rotated. Right now, some of our sheep are feeding off the grass here. Hop in the truck and I'll show you the rest of our property."

As Niall drove Larry around, he described how pastures were rotated, with an eye on grass height and overall pasture health and sustainability, how fences and gates were routinely inspected and maintained, how sheep were weighed and inspected for hoof health, parasites, and other health concerns. By the time they returned to the house, Larry's head was spinning with all the information he'd been given.

"That's quite an operation they have, isn't it?" He commented as he and Aidan filled travel mugs with coffee and headed out to visit Derry.

"Niall told me once their flock used to be larger, but his father lost a significant number of sheep in a bad foot and mouth disease outbreak followed by a harsh winter several years back."

"Is Mr. Donoghue over his cancer? I thought he looked a little pale this morning."

Aidan had noticed the same thing several times in the past few months. "Niall says he's fine. Niall would tell me if anything was going on." As he drove, though, Aidan whispered a prayer for the elder Donoghue's health.

Larry hesitated to ask the next question but decided to continue as he and Aidan were already touching on serious topics. "Is it hard for you to watch Niall and his father together when your own father is gone?"

Aidan felt the wall he'd built to keep his memories and emotions in check rise once again. "Once in a while it hits me, but not as often anymore. I've grown used to it." Alright, it wasn't full truth, he admitted to himself; there were times he wished he could share a tea with his father the way Niall could, or fish for trout with his father on the nearby Owenkillew River, or play music with his father late in the evening as the sun slipped behind the horizon and night settled in. Circumstances could not be changed, he knew. He'd accepted that and most days was fine; there were times, though, such as now, he had to set up barriers to stop memories from flooding in, the only way he could maintain composure.

As they entered Derry's city limits, Aidan told Larry, "I'll start our tour with the area where I grew up. This used to be my father's shop. Here's where Jeannie and I both went to school, and here was our church. And here," he slowed his car to a crawl and pointed a house out, "is where my family and I lived."

His grandmother, he knew, would not have let the shrubs in front grow so out of control, and would already have trimmed the roses for better blooming come summer. He thought the windows could use a good cleaning, and worried that the front door needed a fresh paint job.

Surprised to find the view in front of him had blurred, Aidan knew his emotions were being drawn down too sad a path; he accelerated the car and drove on past the house, turning a corner at the next street, and circling back around the city.

The city Aidan drove them around was small by American standards, Larry thought. The streets were tighter, buildings and shops closer together, and most of the buildings looked so much older than what he was used to. The row houses that lined some streets intrigued him, as did the solid stone arches their car passed under.

"These are the city walls," Aidan explained. "Derry is the only remaining fully walled city in Ireland. Four hundred years old, they are, built in the early sixteen hundreds to protect new English and Scottish settlers. The arches we drove under are called gates; in ancient times huge wooden doors, or gates, would have been fit into those archways and could be closed and bolted against enemy forces."

They drove around the Diamond, the point in the middle of the old city where Bishop Street, Butcher Street, Shipquay, and Ferryquay Streets all intersected, with its tall War Memorial statue, and past the terra cotta colored Guildhall. Aidan then parked his car and led Larry up a set of stone steps to the top of the wall they had driven under. "From here we can get a bird's eye view of the city."

As they progressed along the wall walkway, Aidan related the city's key historical events, from the establishment of a monastery by St. Colmcille in the sixth century, to the Ulster Plantation when English and Scottish settlers moved to Derry, touching on the Troubles but not wanting to dwell on that time.

"How do the Protestants and Catholics here get along now?"

"The battle lines weren't along religion itself," Aidan informed Larry. "It was about treatment of the Irish, who happened to be primarily Catholic, by the British, who were largely Protestant, or more correctly, the Irish Nationalists, who believed Northern Ireland was and should be forever a part of Ireland itself, versus the Loyalists, who felt Northern Ireland should remain a permanent part of Britain. The prejudism and mistreatment of one side by the other grew and grew until it boiled over. My parents suffered through much more of the Troubles than I did. Oh, the stories my father could have told you. My parents and grandmother witnessed so much of it."

Aidan paused, not wanting to relive such turbulent times. "Most people here don't want any more of the fighting. Our history is complex, like the Celtic knots Ireland is famous for. My city has survived some hard times, but she's come through it all and is that much stronger for it."

By now they had stepped down from the walls and stood at the foot of the Peace Bridge. "This bridge was opened in 2011 as a way of joining the two sides and fostering the peace most of us want now."

Walking to the middle of the bridge, Larry gazed out on the

river flowing underneath, gauging from the ripples spreading over the steely blue surface and the breeze that played against his jacket that the water would be quite cold to the skin. He admired the landscape on both sides, and the houses and businesses visible from the bridge, and wondered how far the river wound around the curve beyond where he could see.

Aidan watched the sun reflecting off the ripples of water like so many diamonds. Around him the city he'd grown up in bustled with new growth and fresh facelifts on older buildings. A positive vibe flowed out of the city inspired, he liked to think, by the opening of the Peace Bridge he stood upon. He hoped the peace agreement currently in place would hold and the future would continue to look bright for his beloved city.

They stopped in one of Derry's pubs for a quick pint before heading home. Larry enjoyed listening to the banter between patrons at the bar, and the easy ambiance inside the pub. Aidan told him stories about some of the people he recognized, and recounted some of his own experiences at the pub. As they talked, the bartender came over from behind the bar.

"Aidan O'Connell, could that be you?"

"Hey there, Barry! Good to see you!"

"You as well. How are you keeping these days?"

"Fair, and you?"

"Not too bad. Where have you been keeping yourself these days? We don't see you much, now you've moved away."

"I've been that busy with the band the last while I don't get into town as much anymore."

"And how's that band of yours doing?"

"We're a little slow at the moment," Aidan admitted.

"Then get yourself in here to play a night or two!"

Before they left, Aidan had agreed to perform at the pub two nights in the coming month.

"You have a lovely city," Larry commented as Aidan guided their car back home. "I enjoyed learning the history and seeing the places you grew up around."

"Next time we visit there I won't drag you to so many of the personal history spots," Aidan promised. "There's still plenty to see there and more pubs to check out."

"Is it hard for you to go back to Derry?"

Aidan didn't answer right away. He kept his eyes focused on the road ahead, anxious to return to the house he occupied now and put old ghosts to rest. He hadn't minded the trip to Derry, but as he drove home he had to admit to himself it had stirred more memories than he'd thought it would. "I've learned the art of keeping a distance between myself and my memories," he told Larry at length, knowing it was a partial truth at best.

"Are you sure we're doing the right thing?" Pauline hesitated beside Niall's car, all of a sudden afraid that a trip to her parents' house might not be a good idea. "You know they won't be any less angry than they were when they first found out."

"I know." Niall held the door open, watching as she slid into the car. "We should try, though. We have to end this stalemate."

Daniel O'Shea glanced up at the sound of a car pulling into his driveway, dropped the tire he was installing on his truck, and stormed inside.

"Go away," he shouted when Niall knocked on the door.

Niall pleaded, "We'd just like to talk for a minute."

"You've got nothing to say that we want to hear! You've shamed our family."

"He hasn't shamed me, Da," Pauline called out. "We're going to be married."

"I know we didn't handle all of this the the way you would have wanted," Niall added, "but I love your daughter and I'll take good care of her and our baby."

"You've had your say," Mr. O'Shea shouted back. "Now get out of here!"

Feeling that they'd made a start, that Mr. O'Shea had at least heard and would now think over what they had said, Niall grasped Pauline's arm and pulled her away. "Let it go for now, love. In time he'll come around."

"He won't, though," she insisted. "I know what he's like. He'll never forgive me!"

"I guarantee you when he looks into the eyes of his first grandchild, everything else we've done will be forgiven." Niall started their car and backed out the driveway.

"I'm telling you, Niall, it won't be. I've known him all my life, you've only been around him a few short years. I've always been the one out of all his children to do whatever he said, to never cause him any trouble. Now I've let him down, I've betrayed him. He'll not let go of his anger for a very long time."

Niall drew his eyes off the road long enough to glance at Pauline, so beautiful in the new mint green dress his mother had treated her to, her dark hair fastened back with a silver clip, the silver trimmed Connemara marble earrings and necklace he'd given her for Christmas sparkling at her ears and throat. He was furious that her father could be so cold to her, so damned unforgiving. His anger would serve no purpose though, he thought.

Praying he was right, he told Pauline, "I'm sure he'll soften in time. For now, let's just focus on our baby and the life we're building together. I promise you, it will all work out fine in the end."

"You're quiet tonight," Larry observed as he and Aidan arrived back at Aidan's house.

"I'm sorry. I guess I have too much on my mind."

"That trip down memory lane was harder than you thought it would be."

"That's part of it." Aidan unlocked the door to his house. "Care for a pint?" He opened two bottles and motioned for Larry to follow him out to the bench by the lough that separated Aidan's and Niall's properties.

"Can I ask you something?" When Aidan nodded, Larry proceeded, "This morning you mentioned you hadn't talked to Fionna much in the past couple of weeks. Is that what's bothering you?"

"It is, more than I thought it would. You know me; in all our recent tours didn't I take time almost every day to call Fionna and see how she was?"

"You did," Larry agreed.

"Right. I always took time to connect with her. I know she's in a new city, there's so much exciting stuff to see and do, and her art assignments keep her busy as well, but I would have thought she'd have a little more contact with me anyway."

"She's going through a lot of changes right now."

"Everything's changing. Niall's getting married, Patrick and Moira have their hands full with their kids, Michael's gone solo …". Aidan paused, then continued, "I'm happy for Niall. I always knew he'd end up with Pauline, and he'll be a phenomenal dad. Patrick can't help the health issues Eamon is facing, but I don't know how he'll manage carrying on with the band. Michael has always wanted the solo career he's now pursuing. And Fionna, honest to God, I want her to be successful. She's got the talent, she works hard, she deserves success.

"But it feels like everything around me is falling away, the

131

sand underneath my feet is shifting so fast I'm losing my foothold, and it's hard, it's scary, and I'm feeling lost."

Larry understood. The last few months, with the divorce he'd gone through, he'd found himself lost so many days and nights he could no longer count. Even now his footing was shaky at best. "I can't tell you how to get through these days," he spoke, his words sounding insignificant against the magnitude of Aidan's problems. "I can only tell you to hang on. You made it through a very hard year not too far back. If you could get through that as well as you did, you can make it through what you're facing now."

They sat in silence a while, finishing their pints, each wrapped in his own thoughts. For Larry, the future that had lain so empty before him when his divorce was final, when he'd been forced to find new lodging, and then the tour cancellation and months ahead with no job, nothing to keep him grounded, now had meaning and structure as Aidan and the Macready's boys filled his days.

The anxiety that had gnawed inside Aidan for days settled a bit with Larry's words. As he finished his drink, Aidan studied the stars overhead. The Milky Way's swath of millions of stars shone clearer than it had in weeks. He thought once again of his grandmother's deep faith. If the hand that held the Milky Way in place over eons of time could still keep it intact now, perhaps that same hand would help him through the uncertainty that swirled around him.

Dennis studied the three new works Fionna presented. "Your capture of night light is excellent, your use of shadow, especially with the library lions, how you reflected light off the street musician's saxophone, these are very well done. I like the human elements you've added as well. These paintings draw emotions out of viewers. You've done an exceptional job."

Still not fully confident of her abilities in a class with so many talented artists, Dennis's praise made Fionna feel like she did truly belong in the group, she wasn't just filling an open space in the program. "Thank you," she answered. "This assignment was a challenge, it forced me to take on a subject, nighttime, that I hadn't approached before."

"Would you say, then, you're satisfied with what this program has brought you so far?"

As Fionna answered, Dennis focused more on her glowing eyes, shining hair, smooth skin, the softness of her voice, her lilting accent, almost forgetting her words. He wanted her, pure and simple. He would have to move with care, though, so he didn't scare her off.

"Are you free after class? I thought we could grab some coffee and explore the city more. I'd like to show you Little Italy, or The Village. It might give you more inspiration for future assignments."

It never occurred to Fionna to ask if other program participants would join them, or if he took other students places to help their artwork. She enjoyed the brightly colored buildings, the aromas of various foods, the snippets of conversations around her, and Dennis's knowledge of the city's individual districts. He would not let her pay for food or beverages; at times he placed a protective hand on her arm and led her through crowds, his touch feeling warm and reassuring. Thoughts of Aidan faded further into the folds of her mind, the instructor guiding her through so many new, exciting things now held her attention.

11

Michael spent the morning as he had the past couple of weeks, practicing over and over his parts to the duets Diarmid had offered him. In one he held the more prominent melody lines, in the other he deferred more of the melody to Bridget. In his practicing, Michael focused first on the song where he had the lesser voice, then spent more of his day on the song where he had the larger role.

Some parts of the songs he had down, other sections he had to sing repeatedly. After hearing him run through the same sections day after day for days on end, Susannah was ready to throw something at him, the water bottle in her hand, perhaps, or her whole damn laptop! The veins along her temples throbbed, her jaw ached from clenching her teeth so tight, she couldn't buy a clear thought for all she had racing through her mind, and Michael's repetition of the same words and notes over and over again just about made her mind snap in two.

If she were honest with herself, Susannah would admit the fault wasn't Michael's. Her nerves were on edge anyway. The Morgans' fiftieth anniversary party she'd been hired to plan was not falling into place the way most of her events had; she'd tried three venues, two of them were booked, the third was damaged by a kitchen fire three days after she'd signed a contract to use it, and every other day the sons and daughters throwing the party wanted the menu changed, the color scheme changed, the guest list added to or subtracted from.

Then there were the proposals she'd written up for two other events, a twenty-fifth anniversary celebration for a retail shop she'd arranged events for in the past, and a groundbreaking party for a new commercial office building. She'd spent days poring over every detail of her proposals, analyzing, fine tuning, tweaking until each was perfect for the client and event proposed, only to lose out in the end to her competitors.

As if that wasn't enough, her mind kept returning to the thin box in her purse, and all it represented. She withdrew it from her purse now and, hands shaking, read for the dozenth time the instructions on the side of the box.

Her conscience told her she should let Michael know what she was about to do, give him a chance to be a part of the moment. Her heart, though, listened to his intense practicing, understood the stress he was under, and was reluctant to add to his worries.

Signing on with Diarmid Fitzsimmons had been a huge boost to Michael, but now he had to prove himself to his producer and to the audience he hoped to draw in. Always a perfectionist when it came to music, Michael was now pushing himself harder than ever. Susannah could hear him call himself names, berate himself for not getting a note right, even hit the desk or wall closest to him out of frustration.

No, there was no sense adding to his stress until she knew for sure what she was dealing with.

Dennis drew Fionna aside as she entered class ahead of the others. "Are you free for coffee after class? I have an opportunity for your artwork I'd like to discuss with you."

Intrigued, Fionna agreed to his request.

After the other students had left, Dennis escorted Fionna to his favorite small coffee shop around the corner from Gatewood. He ordered a salted caramel mocha and a slice of apple pie from the pastry case that ran alongside the counter. She studied the beverage menu, overwhelmed by so many selections, and just chose hot tea.

"Anything else?" The cashier asked.

Fionna glanced at the offerings behind the clear glass. The scones in particular tempted her, reminding her of home, but she'd spent more on canvas and brushes last week than she had planned and hesitated to spend any unnecessary money now.

"My treat," Dennis offered, which Fionna found impossible to turn down.

Three empty tables stood alongside the wall of the narrow café. Dennis led Fionna to the one farthest to the back, pulled a chair out for Fionna, and seated himself across from her.

"You're doing very well in class," he told her. "Not that I'm surprised, we chose you for this scholarship based on the high quality of your work and your passion for art. Still, you take my criticisms and suggestions to heart, don't push back against what I say, and you improve your abilities every week."

"I love your critiques." Fionna shook her head and gave a light laugh. "Well, maybe love isn't the right word! I value them, though. I'm here to learn."

"Where do you want your artwork to go? What are your dreams?"

"I want to advance in the world of art, to improve, and to gain more exposure."

"You're repeating the words you used when we interviewed you." Dennis pointed to his own heart. "I want to know what your heart says. I want to hear your dreams."

Fionna carried so many dreams in her heart she sometimes struggled to separate them out. She dreamed of the day she would see pride shining in her parents' eyes as they viewed her artwork on display. True, she'd seen glimpses of that at times, but she wanted more, she wanted them to beam with pride, not just send a few smiles her way.

She dreamed of Aidan, of building a life with him, of sharing her future with him. Moving into his house had been the first step towards realizing that dream. Someday, when her art studies and shows had settled down, she would join him again. Right now, though, she had to grab the opportunities that came her way, make the most of them, reach for all that she could with her art.

That was her biggest dream, and the one she shared with Dennis now. "I want to show my artwork in all the best galleries in New York, London, and Europe. I want my name to be the biggest draw in the art world, the buzz on people's lips, the star of the show."

Dennis watched Fionna's face light up as she spoke of her artwork dreams, how her emerald eyes shone like the jewels they matched, how her whole body became animated as she shared her passion, her dreams, with him. Of all the students at Gatewood this season, he knew he'd selected the right one for what he was about to present.

"As you know," he started now, "in addition to individualized instruction, we offer opportunities to share our students' works with various art collectors and gallery owners. In a couple weeks we will be hosting a private showing for several gallery owners and art critics from San Francisco, Paris, and London. We'd like to display your artwork for them."

Fionna couldn't catch her breath. This was the break she'd hoped for! Now it was here, and she found herself so overwhelmed she couldn't speak. She stared at Dennis, forgetting her manners for a moment, then shook her mind clear and responded, "Dennis, I would love that! I'd be thrilled to have my works shown to them."

Dennis smiled, a broad grin that matched the light in his eyes. "I knew it, I knew you were the right person. Fionna, let me be the one to open the door to your dreams! I can connect you with the right people. I can help you reach the top of the art world."

As he spoke, Dennis took hold of Fionna's hands. Caught off guard, her first reaction was to pull her hands free. She resisted that urge; not wanting to upset her instructor and mentor, she allowed him to hold both of her hands for a couple of minutes before he released them.

For the rest of the evening, as they discussed which of her works to display, which art critics were scheduled to attend, which art galleries would send representatives, Dennis forced himself to keep a respectable distance, to not let the glimmer in Fionna's eyes send his pulse racing, to ignore the fragrance of the perfume she wore. He must not make his move too soon, before she was fully primed. He walked her back to her apartment building, watching as she unlocked the building's front door then was gone, a cloud of copper hair disappearing behind frosted glass. As he walked back to his own place, her perfume and smile walked with him.

The sound of his mobile phone ringing woke Aidan. Three-forty showed on the phone's screen, along with Fionna's name.

"Hello?" He called into the phone, hoping the phone hadn't rung too long, hoping he hadn't missed her.

"Aidan?" Fionna called back. "Are you there?"

"Yes. What's wrong? Are you okay?"

"I'm fine! I'm sorry I'm calling in the middle of your night; I just couldn't wait. I have some fantastic news!"

"What's that?" Aidan was more awake now, relieved there was nothing wrong, wondering what news couldn't wait for a better hour.

"They're going to show my works at a private showing, with critics and gallery people from San Francisco, London, and Paris!"

Half asleep when he first answered Fionna's call, her announcement jolted him awake. He understood at once the full implications of what her news meant. Visions of Fionna jetting from one art capital to another in a continual circle around the globe swept over him like a heavy ocean wave threatening to drown him in its undertow. Aidan had no doubt she would do well in the upcoming showing. Her talent called out from her artwork with the same magnetic draw as her personal presence and charisma did. She would captivate them all, her star would rise and shine bright, and he would lose her.

"I have so much to do, Aidan! I don't know which paintings to show. I wish you were here to help me sort through them."

Fionna's words snapped Aidan back from his visions to her presence on the other end of the phone. "Your instructors at the art school will guide you," he reminded her. "Listen to them and listen to your heart. You'll know which ones to choose."

Aidan forced himself then to pay attention as Fionna described what she thought the show would be like, what Dennis had said about her work and talents, her excitement for how she might be on a fast track for international acclaim causing her words to rush out as if they were desperate to beat her to Europe. As she poured out her hopes and fears, he held back any comments about his concerns for their future. This was not the time for that discussion.

By the time they ended their call Fionna was calmer and ready to relax, while Aidan, now fully awake, knew sleep for the night was over for him. He tiptoed downstairs, brewed tea, then took his steaming mug and one of the scones from Mrs. Donoghue's latest batch into his study.

His sister, Jeannie's painting of a Donegal beach stood on an easel in a corner of the room. As he studied it, he wondered what would have become of her if she had lived. Would she have risen in the art world as Fionna was now? Jeannie had been so talented, he had no doubt she would have had a career in art. If she had wanted that, he thought. She had died so young she hadn't had time to formulate what she wanted out of life.

At least Fionna knew what she wanted and was reaching for her goals. Aidan wanted her to succeed, he truly did. He could see what would happen next, though. Fionna would be a hit at the private showing, she'd be invited to London, or Paris, and would be away for longer stretches.

Fionna's moving into his house had been one of Aidan's dreams. She was the breath of fresh air his life had needed. More than that, she was the vision and voice that caused his heart to skip a few beats then race ahead to try to catch up with itself. In Fionna he'd found a new purpose; his days no longer revolved only around a drive to create music, now he also felt a desire, no, need, to try to create a world that would entice Fionna to want to join her future with his for more than just a period of time. His plans had started to venture into the long-term realm. His mind had even dared to whisper the word "forever" to his heart.

He hadn't foreseen her art taking such a meteoric trajectory, at least not this soon.

Aidan watched the light outside shift from night black to slate grey, to a purplish, bluish grey, to misty silver. He watched the sun appear through and then over the line of trees that marked the edge of his property, ribbons of pink and gold turning to cream, and then soft blue. He watched songbirds cast brief shadows across the sky as they flew in search of food. He heard Farley, the Donoghues' dog, bark and the echo of doors closing as morning on the sheep farm was underway.

The world around him moved forward as it always did, as if no sudden break in its turning had occurred, as if its moorings had not just been yanked free and it now drifted aimlessly through cosmic space. His world alone had been cast into an uncertain orbit, a feeling he hated, the fear of which he tried to quell now with normal morning activities of brewing coffee and frying bacon and eggs as Larry joined him for breakfast.

Nervous didn't even begin to cover what Michael felt as he met with Bridget in the room Diarmid had set aside for rehearsing. One of the top five female singers in Ireland, Bridget's music had inspired him for the past decade; standing in the same room with her now was both exhilarating and intimidating. For the first ten minutes he had to remind himself to take deep, full breaths, to slow his words as he spoke to her, to focus on the work at hand and not the fact that he stood next to one of his musical heroes.

"I'll be honest with you," Bridget leveled with Michael after their initial run through of the first song, "when Diarmid first mentioned you I wasn't too keen. I wasn't familiar with your music. I was wrong, though. You have a powerful voice. You've got a nice tone, not forced, but clear and strong. I think we'll do fine together."

"Thank you." He intended to say more, had a string of words prepared in his mind, but he remained awestruck, silent beyond those two words.

As they worked, though, fine tuning passages here and there

in both songs, trading suggestions for ways to improve their parts, Michael forgot his starstruck shyness and interacted with Bridget more as though they were equals, on par with each other, two singers focused on perfecting the material they worked on so the songs would shine for their audience.

"I think we have two winners here, Michael." Bridget folded her sheet music closed and rose to collect her coat and handbag. "Diarmid was right to team us together. It's a pleasure working with you."

"It's an honor to work with you." Michael rose and shook Bridget's hand. "If our recording tomorrow goes as well as our rehearsal, I agree; I think we have two hits here."

Susannah's hands shook as she opened the box, read and reread the instructions, and prepared herself for the outcome. She held her hopes in check; she'd felt positive before, only to be disappointed. Even though her condition seemed different this time, her stomach queasy each morning, her period delayed ten weeks, her symptoms might be more stress and less what she hoped for.

With meticulous care she followed the steps, waited the allotted time, then closed her eyes, took three deep breaths, opened her eyes and read the test results.

Positive! She was pregnant! The fact that she read the test alone, that she hadn't so much as hinted to Michael about her condition, faded from her mind. She wouldn't blurt out her news the minute he walked through the door. She would wait a few more days, until his recording sessions with Bridget were through. She'd then prepare a special dinner for him, using the set of Belleek china they'd received as a wedding present, and the Waterford wine glasses they had purchased to celebrate their last anniversary, and reveal the results sometime between the main course and dessert.

12

"Mind you take everything you need with you; you'll not be coming back here this night." Anna scanned the items in Niall's overnight bag. "Your shoes! Where are the shoes to go with your good suit?"

"Already over to Aidan's along with the suit." Niall took the hairbrush from his mother and slid it into the side of his bag. "I don't see why I have to spend the night there."

"It's bad luck to see your bride before the wedding."

Niall laughed. "Mam, I've seen Pauline every day since she moved in here! Sure, one more night wouldn't doom us."

"All the same, hurry, gather the rest of your things and be gone with you! And be sure to take the peach cobbler I made for you and Aidan."

Niall did as he was told, knowing there were times arguing with his mother would do no good.

After he was gone, Anna hurried downstairs with the piece of paper he'd given her and dialed the number he'd written out.

"Helen? This is Niall's mother, Anna. Is your man about?"

Helen O'Shea felt everything inside her stiffen. "He's off to the pub for a while. You'll not catch him tonight."

"Don't hang up!" Anna lowered her voice so Pauline, relaxing in a luxurious lavender bubble bath, wouldn't hear her. "It's you I want to speak with. You know your Pauline is marrying our Niall tomorrow, don't you?"

Helen remembered the simple invitation, white embossed lettering on white card stock, Daniel had tossed in the refuse bin, which she'd later retrieved and hidden in her dresser drawer. "Yes, I'm aware."

"Are you planning to attend?"

"Did you honestly think we would?"

Anna, knowing her time was short before Pauline came downstairs, went right to the point. "You're her mam! Don't you care to see your daughter on the most important day of her life? Do you know she was in tears this evening, wanting so badly to have you be a part of her special day?"

True, the lass hadn't cried, but Anna was desperate and prayed God would forgive a small lie.

Helen let the hard edge inside her slip away. "Anna, I don't know what I can do. I want to be with my daughter in the worst way. My Daniel, though, won't hear of it. I don't know how I can go against him."

Anna never could understand how a woman could let herself be ruled by a man against her wishes. Thankful she'd married Will, whose orders were so much bluff and bluster and who, in the end, almost always let her have her way, she could only tell Helen, "I don't have any answers for you. I only know if it was my daughter about to be married Cú Chulainn himself couldn't keep me away."

Anna terminated the call then. Let the woman think things over, she told herself, praying her phone call would work some kind of magic.

Pauline stared out the window at the soft morning mist filling the space between the Donoghues' house and Aidan's where, in a few short hours, she and Niall would be married.

"Why couldn't the sun have cut its way through just this once?" she lamented.

Will studied the skies. "It's brightening, child. By the time the afternoon is here, you'll have the sun smiling down on you."

Anna poured fresh tea for herself and Pauline. "Come, love, let's start getting you all made up. Will, see who that is knocking at our door. If it's our Niall, send him away!"

Will opened the door to find a woman in a fine green dress.

"Mr. Donoghue, I'm Helen O'Shea, Pauline's mother. Might I come in?"

"Mam?" Floored, Pauline watched her mother enter the living room, while Anna whispered a prayer of thanks. "Is my dad here as well?"

"No, he's home. I just couldn't stay away, this being your wedding day."

Happy her phone call had worked, Anna handed her cup of tea over to Helen. "Here, you two take your drinks upstairs. Pauline can show you around; I'll join you in a few minutes."

Pauline showed her mother the room she now shared with Niall and the room they would turn into a nursery. When Anna joined them, they showed Helen the dress they'd found in Omagh, cream colored silk with a minimal touch of lace, tea length, with capped sleeves and a sweetheart neckline.

Helen and Anna helped Pauline dress and fix her makeup. Pauline chose to leave her hair down, the way Niall liked it best. As she brushed it smooth, Anna handed her a box.

"I picked these up the day we bought your dress. I thought they'd give your hair a bit of a special touch."

Inside the box, Pauline found twin hair clips studded with pearls and rhinestones.

"They're gorgeous!" Pauline remembered the day she and

Anna had gone dress shopping, how they'd enjoyed a special tea after and solidified their relationship. "Anna, thank you. I love these, and I love you."

Pauline fixed the clips on either side of her hair, added a final touch of blush to her makeup, then stood before her full-length mirror and studied her reflection, smoothing the silk over her stomach, grateful the dress hid what lie underneath.

Helen stepped behind her, smoothed Pauline's hair, placed her hands on her daughter's shoulders, and whispered, "You look so beautiful. You need a touch of jewelry, though." She pulled a blue velvet box from her purse. "My mother gave me these on my wedding day. You should have them now."

Hands shaking, guessing what the box contained, Pauline opened it to find a delicate pearl necklace and earrings. "Oh Mam, your special set! I can't take these."

"You can, and you will." Removing the necklace from its box, Helen fastened it around Pauline's neck, added the earrings, then stood back for her daughter to see.

"Pretty as a picture, you are." Anna wiped tears from her eyes. "We best be going now before we all need to re-do our mascara!"

They could have walked across the grass to Aidan's house, but Will insisted on driving them so Pauline wouldn't ruin her delicate cream shoes. Aidan and Mack met them at the front door.

"You look stunning!" Aidan complimented as Pauline stepped inside. "I better get back to Niall. He's a nervous wreck! There's coffee and pastries in the kitchen if you want a little something. Mack will take care of anything you need. I'll see you all in a bit."

"Was that Pauline at the door?" Niall demanded when Aidan returned to the study where they both waited for the wedding to begin. "How is she doing? Does she look very pretty?"

Never one to pass up an opportunity for fun, Aidan turned a deadpan face towards Niall. "Aye, that was her, coming over to tell me she's changed her mind about marrying you. She's gone now."

"What?" Panicked, Niall dashed for the door to catch Pauline and bring her back.

"Don't bother!" Aidan stopped him. "I was having the craic with you! She's here she's fine, for some reason she insists on going through with this despite my best attempts to persuade her to see sense."

"Damn you!" Niall flung his arm out to swat at Aidan, smacked his wrist against the edge of the desk near him, and clutched at his arm, grimacing in pain.

Aidan laughed all the more at Niall's mishap. "Hope you haven't broken your arm just before your wedding night!"

"If I have it's down to you! I hope you feel horrible!"

Their banter was interrupted by Patrick opening the door. "It's time."

Niall turned back to Aidan, "This is it. I'm doing the right thing, aren't I?"

"You are indeed." Aidan squared himself in front of Niall, straightened his best friend's tie, placed his hands on Niall's shoulders, and leveled his most serious look at Niall. "Pauline's a lovely lass. Together, you're a perfect team. You're going to have the most beautiful baby in the world, and you'll both be brilliant parents."

Aidan, Patrick, and Larry had decorated the grand ballroom in Aidan's house with red rose garlands and red, cream, and white bows and ribbons tucked amid multiple strands of fairy lights. At one end of the room rows of folding chairs had been set up for the small gathering. At the other end stood two long folding tables laden with sandwich platters, casserole dishes, and a wedding cake with white frosting and red roses cascading down the sides.

Niall and Aidan took their places at the head of the room. When Pauline entered, escorted by Mack, Niall felt the whole room light up. He watched her face shine as she walked the short white carpet runner to where he stood and felt her hand tremble the slightest bit as he tucked it into his own, realizing that his, too, was shaking.

The ceremony took less than twenty minutes, officiated by a minister friend of Aidan's. Kate, as matron of honor, and Mack, who gave the bride away, both beamed as if Pauline were their own daughter. Niall and Pauline read short vows they each had written, and exchanged rings Conor and Caitlyn had carried in.

"They certainly look the happy couple," Michael noted as he, Susannah and Aidan enjoyed wine and sandwiches after. "She's a radiant bride."

"She is that. They're so well suited for each other."

"They are. Thanks for inviting us. We would have hated to miss this."

Aidan sent a conspiratorial wink to Susannah, and told Michael, "Niall really wanted you here, said you were family. I tried to tell him once you were out of the group you were out of the picture, but he insisted ...". Aidan laughed at Michael's all too hurt look. "You can't take a joke any better than Niall! We would never have not invited you."

Michael had to laugh as well. "I see you haven't lost your penchant for teasing! It's good to see you all. I know I left you all without a proper goodbye. I'm sorry for that."

"We understood," Aidan lied, even though Michael's sudden

departure still hurt more than he wanted to admit. "How is it working with Diarmid?"

"Fine," Michael lied, not wanting to say he was relegated to background vocals and a couple of duets whose recordings had been delayed twice in the past week. "What about you and the rest of the band? I heard your American tour fell through."

"You know how it is. New acts come along, there's a lot of demand for them, festival organizers only have so much money to work with. Once we get a new album out, we'll be back on top."

"Is your new singer here? I'd like to meet him and warn him about you lot!"

"He had a commitment back home and couldn't be here." Aidan studied Susannah. "Michael being home more must agree with you, you look amazing!"

Aidan's comment prompted Michael to take a closer look at her as well. "He's right. You do look lovely. There's something different about you the past few days. It's not your hair . . .".

Susannah had been waiting for the right moment to tell Michael her news, but each night since she'd taken the home test he'd returned from his rehearsals excited, gushing over how brilliant Bridget was, how patient, how talented; he'd eaten a hasty meal each night then holed himself up in the office room preparing for the upcoming days of recording, returning home dejected the two times their recording sessions had been delayed. She'd had little room or time to break her news to him.

This wasn't the time or place she'd pictured, but she couldn't hold off any longer. "Aidan, would you mind if we went through to your living room for a minute?"

"Go on through. Take all the time you need." Aidan waved them on and turned his attention back to the party.

"What is it?" Curious, Michael followed Susannah through to the living room and sat down next to her.

"For the past several days I've wanted to tell you something, but the right time never presented itself. You've had so much going on with your music and all. This isn't the time or place I wanted, but I don't want to hold my secret close any longer."

By now, terrified Susannah was about to tell him she had devastating news, Michael was frantic. "Good God! You're scaring me! Just tell me what it is."

Bracing herself for Michael to be less than excited, she told him, "I'm pregnant."

Michael was speechless for a moment. "That's it? You couldn't tell me that?"

"I wanted to. You've been under so much stress with Diarmid and your recordings, though, and we hadn't planned for this just now, and I didn't know how you'd react."

Ashamed that Susannah didn't feel she could come to him with any matter, large or small, Michael took her hands in his own and apologized. "I'm sorry if I've ever made you feel you couldn't talk to me. Have I really been that bad?"

"No, it's my fault more than yours. I held my news because I didn't want to add to your stress."

"You've never worried about that before."

"I've never been pregnant before."

The reality of Susannah's news sank in, and Michael grinned. "A baby is it then? We're going to be parents?"

Relieved that she'd released her secret at last, Susannah beamed. "We are. You're okay with that, then?"

"Okay? I'm over the moon! Let's go tell the lads!"

Susannah pulled Michael back. "Not tonight. Would you mind keeping this just between the two of us for a few days? I just want it to be our special secret for a bit."

"I want to shout it to the whole countryside," Michael told her. "If it's that important to you, though, alright; we'll do it your way."

"Everything okay?" Aidan asked when Michael and Susannah returned.

Susannah forced herself to suppress a wide smile. "Fine, thanks. I was hoping I'd see Fionna tonight; is she here?"

"She's studying art in New York for a couple of months."

All day Aidan had pushed aside thoughts of Fionna, focusing more on his best friend and his friend's bride. Now he felt a deep cavern open inside his heart. As he glanced around the grand room, he observed Mack and Kate dancing to a slow song the disc jockey he and Niall's parents had hired was playing, their eyes full of love for each other. Michael and Susannah danced together as well, close, sensuous, looking golden, beautiful, successful, and blissfully in love. Patrick and Moira sat at a table with their four kids, Eamon having recovered from his recent heart episode, the six of them deep in conversation, a perfect family unit. Will and Anna were talking with Niall, Pauline and Helen, Will's hand on Anna's back a visible show of the support and closeness they'd exchanged for decades, Niall and Pauline with faces glowing with their new, official commitment of love for each other.

Aidan was desperate for that kind of love in his life. He'd thought he had found it with Fionna. The longer she stayed in New York, though, the more distance he felt between them. He thought again of his last conversation with her and his fear of losing her and wondered anew if she'd return to him at all, or if her ever increasing circle of art connections would lead her further and further away as he imagined. Some situations had no answers; he knew he could only let the future play out as it was meant to.

Larry, surrounded by so many demonstrations of romantic love, thought back to his own failed marriage, guilt flooding through him again as he knew the collapse of it was down to him. He'd been away from home too often and for too long each time. When he was home, he and his wife had taken to communicating through criticism and argument, creating an atmosphere so fraught with tension in the end both parties agreed divorce was the only way either of them could survive. As he watched Niall and Pauline and the other couples around him dance, he wondered if he would ever fall in love again. He immediately discarded the thought. One failed relationship was painful enough. He didn't have the heart to go down that path again.

Watching Niall and Pauline dance, Patrick took Moira's hand in his. "Did we look that over the moon at our own wedding?"

"Worse!" Moira laughed and covered his hand with her free one. "You've looked back at our photos from time to time. We looked like we'd swallowed a full box of sticky toffee, we had such sugary sweet smiles on us!"

"Right, well, give them two a dozen years and a couple of kiddies, and they'll look as tired and stressed as we do now, won't they?"

Patrick had laughed as he spoke those words, but they stung Moira just the same. As tired and worn out as she felt so many days, she hoped she didn't give that impression to the world outside her inner circle. She pulled her mobile phone out of her handbag, opened the photos, and studied the ones they'd taken that morning of herself, Patrick and their children all scrubbed and dressed for the wedding. Relieved, she pushed the photo towards Patrick. "We don't look that worse for wear, do we?"

"I don't know how you do it," Patrick told Moira as he reviewed the photo. "You look after everything with the four of them, deal with me, carry the whole world on your shoulders, and you still come up smiling." The reality of all she dealt with had penetrated through Patrick's mind over the past several days as they'd dealt with Eamon's most recent health crisis, as he'd watched her care for Eamon, juggle Eileen's, Caitlyn's and Conor's needs as well as his own, and do so with so much grace and patience it would have looked to the world at large she was unaffected by it all. He'd also seen her late at night, though, and over cups of tea during the day when the children were all out of earshot, when her stoic front had slipped and she'd snapped at him, or cried an ocean of tears, frustrated, exhausted, and overwhelmed by the responsibilities she carried.

The disc jockey switched from a fast song to a slower ballad. Patrick asked Conor and Caitlyn, "Would you look after your brother and sister for a bit while I dance with your mom?" He held his hand out to Moira, led her to the dance floor, and drew her in close to him. As they circled the floor, he whispered in her ear, "You do know you're the loveliest woman here, don't you?"

"You've had one too many pints, haven't you," she whispered back. Still, she could feel her face glow at his compliment. "If Niall's half as good a husband to Pauline as you are to me, she'll be lucky indeed."

Whenever they had danced in the past, Moira had reveled in the feel of Patrick's hand across her back and his light grasp on her free hand exuding confidence and security, his sensual breath on her neck and ear, the smell of his aftershave lotion; she'd felt well loved and cared for, and thankful that she'd been the one to win Patrick over all the other girls who had set their sights on him.

Today, she felt something else as well. All afternoon she'd felt the bond between the Macready's Bridge members, and how connected all their families were. She'd always felt that when they were all gathered, as they had been when Aidan's family had passed so unexpectedly, as they had when Michael and Susannah were married, and when Eamon and Eileen were baptized. This time seemed different, somehow. The band was not riding the crest of a wave of success, the wave had flattened out and they were in between swells. With Michael stepping away, and James new to the band, they were navigating rougher waters, not a full-blown storm but a sea that tossed them about more than they were used to.

She remembered how she'd begged so many times in recent weeks for Patrick to stay at home and help her out more, how after Eamon's most recent health emergency Patrick had promised he would step away from the band and be there for her and their children.

"I was wrong," she told Patrick as he spun her around the floor. "I don't want you to be home. I want you to stay with the band."

Caught by surprise, Patrick stopped mid-step. "What are you saying?"

"Dance me around a bit more so people won't notice we're talking," she whispered. He complied, and as they circled the floor she explained, "I want you around, yes, and I'm frightened and overwhelmed whenever I face a crisis. But Patrick, you belong with the band. They need you. You're all going through too much right now for you to leave."

"You need me as well, though, and our children do."

"Kate and I have managed this long. We'll get by."

"Are you sure?" When Moira gave him a tearful nod, he replied, "Alright, I'll stay with them." In his heart, Patrick was relieved; leaving the band was the last thing he had wanted. "Promise me, though, if you have a change of heart you'll discuss it with me, calm and reasonable, and not bludgeon me with it every time I'm home."

Before Moira could protest, Patrick spun her around, dipped her, and they both laughed as they returned to their table.

Before ending the evening, Niall motioned for Aidan to follow him outside. The sky had turned a mixture of dusky blue, heather pink, lavender and gold, all reflected in the smooth water of the lough nearby. He nodded to the lough and the property just beyond it.

"Just a few years ago we learned you owned our property. It almost killed our friendship." He looked over to Aidan. "I'm so glad you didn't let that happen."

"Niall, when I lost my family you and your parents took over and made me part of your clan." A lone bird flew over the lough, headed for its nighttime roosting place. He thought that bird was like him, on its own yet knowing where to find shelter and comfort. "I would be lost without you all."

"We'd never let you go. Thank you for everything you did to help us pull this wedding together in such a hurry. When Pauline and I get back in a couple of days we'll settle up with you for whatever it cost."

"No, you won't. It's all on me. You save your money for things you're going to need for your baby."

Niall started to protest; Aidan held a hand up to stop him. "Don't even start. Just name the baby after me if it's a boy! Now get back in there before your wife thinks you've run off without her!"

Niall found Pauline talking with Mack and Kate, her face animated, her long hair held back at the sides by the hair clips she'd told him his mother had bought her. In a flash he thought back to the night when he'd first met her at The Harp. She'd caught his eye the minute he walked into the pub, and she'd held it ever since. Now, watching her easy, natural way with people, struck once again by her beauty, he had to convince himself that the whole day was real, they were married, he wasn't dreaming.

Niall stepped in and interrupted their conversation. "I'm sorry, but Pauline if we don't leave now we won't get to our bed and breakfast before dark."

"You two get on your way," Mack insisted. "Niall, when you get back we'll talk about where the band's at; I may have a few more bookings sorted by then."

To Pauline, Kate said, "You've married a wonderful man. I hope you both will be as happy as Mack and I are."

After circling the room and saying goodbye to all who had gathered for their wedding, Niall and Pauline finished their evening with Aidan, Will, Anna and Helen.

"You'll look after things while we're gone, right?" Niall asked Aidan.

Aidan winked at Will and Anna and told Niall, "No, I'll be away myself. They'll be fine on their own."

For a moment Niall panicked, then caught the glint in Aidan's eyes. "Stop it! You're a pain in the arse, you know that? You look after my mam and dad, or you'll have me to answer to when I get home!"

Pauline hugged Will and Anna, tears rising in her eyes once again. "Thank you so much for today, for making this such a beautiful day. I'm going to love being part of your family."

Not sure whether he should hug Pauline's mother, or shake her hand, Niall abandoned both and nodded to her instead. "We're so glad you could join us today. You've made Pauline very happy."

"You're the one who's made her happy," Helen corrected. "I'm sorry Daniel and I have been so rough on you. You have my full support going forward."

Pauline wrapped her arms around her mother. "I know it wasn't easy, going against my father today. I'm so happy you did. I hope he doesn't give you too much trouble for it."

Helen pushed a stray hair away from her daughter's face. "Don't you worry your head about that. I can handle him. Now off you go with your Niall. Have a wonderful honeymoon."

They watched Niall and Pauline drive away, then Aidan turned to the Donoghues. "Well, they're off. We gave them a proper wedding, didn't we?"

"You did," Will corrected. "You did all the hard work."

"I just followed the suggestions you both gave me."

Anna surveyed the room they stood in, a faraway look in her eyes. "I always dreamed this room would look this beautiful when I passed it growing up. You didn't just make Niall and Pauline's dream come true today, you made mine as well."

Aidan remembered her telling the story of the house he'd bought, and of this room in particular. "There's one part you've missed out on," he told her now. He whispered something to the disc jockey, pulled out his mobile phone, and nodded to Anna and Will. "There you go. One dance, just the two of you."

Will held his hand out to Anna. "We better not disappoint the boy, or he won't help us out the next couple of days!"

As they glided slowly across the dance floor, Aidan recorded them on his phone so he could show Niall and Pauline later. Thoughts of his parents crowded into his mind; he pushed the thoughts away. Tonight was for joy, not thoughts of loss.

"Where are you taking me?" Pauline asked as Niall drove them outside of Northern Ireland and towards the Connemara region. "You've only told me you had a place reserved at Donegal Town, but that's not where you're heading."

"It's a surprise," was all he would say as he maneuvered their car down highways, over hills, through one small town after another, until he came to signs featuring Corrib and Ashford, and left the highway in favor of narrower roads. An idea came to Pauline, but she was afraid to ask. Only when he crossed a one lane bridge and pulled their car in front of a massive stone edifice did she dare speak.

"Ashford Castle? Oh Niall! You really should have warned me! I haven't brought proper clothes at all for this place. All I have for tomorrow is jeans and a top, nothing fancy!"

"You don't need anything fancy," he assured her. "Even in jeans worn through and a top full of holes you'd be perfect. Besides, I had my mam throw a couple extra bits in your suitcase. You'll be fine."

As they entered the castle, checked in at the desk, and were taken to their room, Pauline gazed around her, taking in as many details as she could of the massive castle-turned-five-star-luxury-hotel, in awe of the centuries' old walkways, the light fixtures and pieces of sterling on display, and the photos that noted the many historical events and guests that were such a large part of Ashford's story.

Their room was a simple one, queen sized bed with a cream and coral color striped duvet, a matching loveseat, and an armchair in a coordinated cream and coral floral fabric. The real showpiece of the room was the view outside their windows of Lough Corrib, whose soft blue waters were rippled by a light breeze and dotted with a dozen or more islands.

"Oh Niall! I can't believe you've arranged this! I won't even ask how much it cost. You could not possibly have given me a better present than this!"

Joining her by the window, Niall put an arm around her shoulders and studied the view along with her. "I remember you once saying how much you dreamed of staying here, how you always wanted to know what it would feel like to be surrounded by so much luxury. I wanted to make that dream come true for you."

They enjoyed the view until dusk fell, that moment called the gloaming when scenery and nightfall blended together and all outside them, minus a light here or there, was one. Checking his watch, Niall directed, "Alright, love, go fix your hair or whatever else you need to tend to. We've got a five-course dinner ahead. Tomorrow we've a boat tour, and a falconry exhibition. And we might have one or two more things to enjoy, this being our honeymoon weekend!"

They both laughed at the suggestiveness in his eyes and tone of voice. As they headed to the dining room, Pauline thought how Niall had made this moment, this whole day, something she'd remember the rest of her life.

13

"Want to give driving here a try?" Aidan asked, tossing Larry the keys to his car while he and Niall packed equipment and suitcases into the car's trunk for their trip to Galway and the first of the twelve gigs Mack had booked for Macready's Bridge.

"No, thank you!" Larry declined Aidan's offer with a laugh. "I've seen your crazy roads!"

"You're up to the challenge," Aidan insisted, refusing to take the keys back.

Larry relented and steeled his nerves as he maneuvered Aidan's car over narrow roads and around blind curves, once almost scraping a stone wall as he pulled the car as far left as possible to avoid an oncoming lorry. Driving a large bus all over America was nowhere near as stressful as this, he thought as he parked the car on the street in front of the pub the band was scheduled for and released his white-knuckle grip from the steering wheel.

Mack, who had driven Patrick and James to Galway, congratulated Larry on surviving his first drive over Irish roads. "Keep learning the roads here, and we'll hire you to be our driver full time."

Still calming his nerves from the close wall experience, Larry wasn't at all sure he wanted that permanent position. On the other hand, the more time he spent at Aidan's home the more he fell under the spell of the countryside around him. Driving for Mack and the band here might be worth an occasional shattering of nerves!

The Thursday night crowd in Galway was thin. Aidan, Patrick, and Niall exchanged disappointed glances in between songs, while James, nervous as he was over his first live show with the band, was relieved the audience was no bigger than any he was used to performing for on his own. For all the cues he'd missed during rehearsals, James hit each of the songs in their first show with precision.

"I wish there had been more people in the audience tonight," James commented as he and Aidan walked back to their cars after the show.

"I'd rather have ten true fans watching us than a hundred people who have no clue who we are."

"What do you mean?"

"Something my father taught me years ago when I would worry about small audiences. It doesn't matter the size of the crowd, just how devoted they are. In time you'll come to appreciate the true fans, the ones who aren't just attending a place they frequent often and you just happen to be performing that night, but the ones who are there because they know they'll see you."

James absorbed the advice Aidan had given him. As they reached their cars, he told Aidan, "Your father sounds like a very wise man."

"He was," Aidan agreed, wishing his father could have been in that Galway pub audience.

In Limerick, the patrons at the pub Macready's Bridge played at were more interested in swapping news and stories with each other and downing pints than they were in any music going on in the background. The Tipperary pub crowd was the same.

Niall, seeing the disappointment James conveyed, tried to reassure him. "Every time we make the rounds of various venues there are some shows where people are focused on every note we play, and some where we're just a backdrop to the social scene surrounding us. Don't worry, we're doing fine."

In his heart, though, Niall struggled to believe the words he'd spoken. Even on their first tour, when Macready's Bridge was unknown, the venues they played at were larger and more geared towards proper concerts than the minor pubs they'd been booked into this time around. He knew Mack was trying his hardest to locate places for the band to play, he had confidence in their manager; but still, if he was honest with himself, he'd have to admit feeling they were scraping the bottom of the barrel with their bookings.

They had two bookings in Cork, both at pubs large enough to have decent band stages and room enough to draw good crowds. The Wednesday night audience was a little thin but attentive. Friday night the pub was packed, the audience cheered and sang along, their enthusiasm infectious, spurring the band to play with fiercer intensity.

In Cobh, the patrons at the pub they were booked in were politely attentive but unenthused, leaving even the usually positive Patrick shaking his head.

"I don't get it," he confided to the others as they packed up their instruments and equipment after the show. "It can't all be because Michael's gone. He couldn't have had that much of a following."

"I can't put my finger on the problem," Niall admitted.

"I don't think it's us." Aidan spotted James to the right of him, knew what the new singer would be thinking, and added, "and James, it's not down to you."

Mack, who had stepped in with Larry to pick up some of their equipment and carry it out to their cars, overheard their conversation and motioned for them all to gather near him.

"I've told some of you this before," he started, "there are times of success in the music field, and there are lean times. You're on a difficult road right now. I wish I could snap my fingers and make it better for you. God knows you're all talented, and you deserve so much more than an unappreciative trickle of people coming out to see you."

Niall checked the schedule on his phone. "We have three shows left, Wicklow and Dublin, right?"

Mack nodded. "Yes. I'm trying for more but haven't had any openings yet."

James read the dismal looks on the faces around him and tried not to let their worries become his own. "This is just a slow time, right? Things are bound to pick up?" He turned to Mack, hoping their manager would give them some positive sign. Instead, Mack leveled a straightforward look at them all.

"There's a lot of competition for the open spots in any pub or venue. I'll keep searching out new openings, though. I haven't given up."

Diarmid Fitzsimmons read through the report in front of him for a third time. There had to be a mistake somewhere in the figures that leapt off the pages and into his brain like electric shocks jolting his senses. He analyzed each line, each column, running calculations in his head and then on his laptop to confirm what the report reflected.

His label had lost an eighth of its profits in the past three months.

"How the hell did this happen?" He demanded of his accountant, known only by his last name, Maguire, when the flushed faced, terrified young man entered Diarmid's office.

"It's all spelled out on page seven," Maguire started to explain. "Excessive spending, investments that didn't work out as expected, taking on too many new projects."

"I can read the report!" Diarmid exploded. "How did you let this happen?"

Maguire knew no matter how he answered he would be blamed for the mogul's downturn; still, he would defend himself no matter how pointless it seemed. "I've sent you several emails with my concerns, and left you two voicemails, all of which have gone unanswered."

"You should have demanded an appointment with me! Go on! Get out of here while I figure out how to pull myself out of this mess!"

Maguire departed, leaving Diarmid to weigh options and choose his best course of action.

Michael and Bridget had taken their places in the recording room, ready to set down at last the duets they had labored over together the past week. Studio musicians had already cut instrumental tracks, the backdrop against which their vocals would shine.

Just as they were about to start, Diarmid stepped in. "Hold up a minute. Michael, can I have a word?"

Fearing this was another last-minute delay in recording, Michael followed Diarmid into the control room. When Diarmid directed the sound engineer to step out of the booth, Michael realized something worse was brewing.

"Michael, we're pulling the duets," Diarmid announced as if he were reporting a weather forecast. "I'm canceling the recording session."

Confused, Michael asked, "You mean just for today, right? You'll reschedule the session?"

Diarmid shook his head. "No, Michael, we've had a

downturn I wasn't expecting. I'm canceling your contract. I have to let you go."

Diarmid was still speaking, but Michael no longer heard the words, his mind reeling, his stomach lurching as if he'd just been dropped down a massive hole in the road.

Now Diarmid was standing, holding out his hand for Michael to shake. "I'm truly sorry, Michael. You have a great talent. I wish you the very best going forward."

Michael shook Diarmid's hand. What else could he do? Diarmid departed, entered the recording room, and broke the news of the duet cancellation to Bridget. Michael left, choosing to avoid any chance of Bridget coming in to console him, to remind him that one setback did not mean the end overall. He could not take her kindness just now.

Catching a taxi, Michael arrived home before midday, much earlier than Susannah had expected.

Susannah felt the first twinge of pain a half hour after Michael left. Fifteen minutes later, the second one hit, sharper and stronger. Within an hour, she was sweating and spotting blood. Before she could call a taxi to take her to the medical clinic, a full-blown hemorrhage hit, gushing more blood than she knew she had in her, leaving her so weak all she could do was lie down on the bathroom's cold tile floor a while. When she felt enough energy return, she made her way to her bed and cried herself to sleep.

Michael was surprised to find the downstairs of their house empty. Most times when he arrived home he would hear Susannah on the phone or typing away on her laptop, or the clattering of pans and dishes as she prepared dinner. Granted, he had returned home earlier than usual, she may have not thought of dinner yet, she might be out on business calls.

We've both worked so hard these past few months, he thought; I'll take Suze out to dinner, one last fling before we tighten our budget until I can find more work.

Running various restaurant options through his mind, Michael climbed the stairs to their bedroom to change his clothes.

"You're home so soon?"

Michael jumped at the sound of Susannah's voice. "Why are you in bed? Are you sick?"

Susannah could not look Michael in the eye; instead, she focused on the Celtic knot pattern stamped across their tan duvet cover. Those knots could be so hard to figure out, she thought. Like them, so many matters in life could be so hard to separate and understand.

"I lost the baby."

The way she said it scared Michael, her tone so flat, so disconnected. If she'd cried, or thrown things or yelled, he would have known how to react. But this, so matter of fact, like their baby had been no more than a side story in their lives, a brief episode, nothing of consequence; that was so not like Susannah he was afraid she'd slipped into some psychological state he would not be able to pull her out of.

Michael crouched next to her side of the bed and placed a supportive hand on her arm. "Tell me what happened."

"There's nothing to tell. I was pregnant. Now I'm not."

"Have you been to the doctor?"

"What for? There's no need now."

"Then how do you . . .". Michael stopped. Even to him the question sounded dumb.

"How do I know?" At last, a spark of emotion flared up in Susannah. "I saw what my body rejected! It was there in all the blood!" Susannah bolted upright, fresh tears flowing. "Oh

Michael, there was so much blood! I never expected that! By the time it stopped, our baby was gone."

Michael sat beside her on the bed and enfolded her in his arms. "Shhh. It's okay. As long as you're okay. You're what matters most. There will be other babies in time."

Susannah let him utter soothing words, no matter how hollow they seemed to her heart. When she could no longer stand the sound of so many empty phrases, she shook his hold free, noticed the time on her nightstand clock, and asked, "Why are you home so early, anyway?"

"Diarmid's canceled my contract. He's dropped me."

"Why would he do that?"

"He said the label's had a downturn. He must be losing a lot of money; I don't think he'd let me go if it was just a mild setback."

"Oh Michael, I'm so sorry. To have that happen, and then come home to this."

"Never mind about me." Michael settled Susannah back against her pillows. "I'm going to bring you some tea, and maybe a bit of that shortbread you like so much. You're to stay in bed the rest of the day. We're going to get through this. You'll see. We'll be fine."

The morning after the Cobh show, Mack, Patrick, Niall, and James headed for Wicklow, while Aidan and Larry stayed behind.

"There's something I want you to see," Aidan told Larry, guiding him around town until they reached a street that ran along water. Larry parked their car, then followed Aidan along a sidewalk to a building with a red flag with white star in the center.

"Do you know what this place is?"

Larry studied the building, nondescript except for the flag, the words "White Star Line" along the top, and "Titanic" in large print over a doorway and on flags alongside the building. He recalled images of the long, sleek luxury liner from his wife and daughter's favorite movie. "They owned the Titanic, didn't they?"

"Aye, they did." Aidan stepped past the building and gazed upon the harbor spread out before them. "Cobh, Queenstown as it was known back then, was the Titanic's last port of call, her last contact with land before she went out to sea." He pointed to a distant spot on the horizon. "She was so massive she couldn't fit in the harbor here, but had to anchor out there where the water was deeper, and people and mail were ferried out to her." After a long silence, he added, "From here, she was never seen again."

Larry tried to imagine the huge ship sitting so far out, receiving her last set of passengers. What must it have felt like as a passenger, boarding such a grand vessel, he wondered. What must it have felt like, the smoothness as the Titanic sliced through the Atlantic's waters, as it struck the infamous iceberg, as it broke and sank.

"All those lives, all those dreams, so much was lost when that ship went down."

Aidan's voice was barely audible. Larry guessed he had more than the tragic ship on his mind. "Kind of like your dreams, right?"

Aidan's gaze remained locked on the invisible luxury liner anchored on the horizon. "I never expected the band would turn a bad corner. We were on such a good trajectory. Everything was working in our favor. Now it seems everything we worked for is slipping away."

Larry had driven buses for enough performers that he

knew the look and feel of bands on the rise and those whose careers were waning. "I've seen bands hit downward spirals and then just as quickly bounce back."

In truth, he hadn't seen them bounce back. Most bands Larry knew did not recover once they hit bottom. He wouldn't tell Aidan that, though. He would rather leave his host friend an element of hope, no matter how tenuous.

Pulling his eyes away from the ghost ship, Aidan smiled at Larry. "Thanks. I hope that's what happens with us."

After a lukewarm experience in Wicklow, Macready's Bridge limped into Dublin, their enthusiasm for their craft hanging by a thin thread. Dublin's crowds were polite, appreciative, but more dedicated to their pints and friends, paying Macready's Bridge no special attention.

Even Michael, who they'd all looked forward to meeting up with, failed to show. "Susannah's not feeling well," he'd told Mack over the phone. "I need to be with her." Michael didn't tell Mack that, with Diarmid having canceled his contract and the days not looking particularly bright as it was, he didn't have it in him to watch his former band succeed where he was failing.

If he'd known how thin the band's turnouts were, he might have felt more like commiserating with them.

"You've done a fine job, boys," Mack congratulated them after their last show had ended, as the venue's patrons filed out. "I'm proud of you all."

Aidan was the first to comment back. "If we did so well, why do I feel such a failure?"

"Same here," Niall agreed.

Patrick, wiping down his fiddle with a soft cloth before tucking it back into its leather case, calculated in his mind his portion of the income from their mini tour, a sum far too low for all the work they'd put in. "Mack, in all honesty, can we turn things around? I don't know how much longer we can go on like this."

Patrick's words echoed the thoughts that had nagged at the back of Mack's mind the past few days. The short run of gigs had been the best he could pull together for the band in transition. While on one hand he still believed he could book more shows for them as James gained more experience and venue owners saw he could pull patrons in, on the other hand they did need to earn enough to support themselves, and in Patrick's case Moira and their children.

"I believe better days lie ahead," Mack told them. "Still, I know your resources won't last forever. Take a week or two off. Think about what you want, what's best for you. Then we'll all meet up and decide our next steps."

14

"You'll be leaving soon." This reality hit Aidan hard. He'd enjoyed Larry's presence for so many weeks and hated the thought of his houseguest returning home. He and Larry had just sat down to relax on new chairs on the flagstone patio they had installed behind Aidan's house. "I've been a horrible host, haven't I? Here you are on your holidays and all I've done is make you work!"

"That was part of the deal," Larry reminded him. "Free room and board as long as I carried my own weight."

"You've sat through days of rehearsals, helped with Niall and Pauline's wedding, driven us around to our recent shows, and done odd jobs around the house here with me. There's nothing on our calendars at the moment. Throw some clothes in a bag, and I'll show you around a bit more of the country before you have to leave."

With overnight bags stashed in the back of Aidan's car, and tea and sandwiches to fuel them, they started off.

"I still don't know how you manage these roads," Larry remarked, impressed, as Aidan maneuvered their car around another blind turn on a one lane winding road. "Even after my turn at driving here, cars coming out of nowhere on these narrow roads still give me a jolt. You can't have any nerves at all!"

"Our cars over here have sensors on them that tell the driver when a car is approaching that we can't see. Didn't I show you that?"

Larry, who thought he knew as much as anyone about cars, had never heard of any sensors like that. "Really?"

Aidan burst out laughing. "No, I was having your leg! There are no sensors. We just drive blindly and pray when we round a corner that we won't meet up close and personal with someone coming from the other way."

Larry grimaced. "I should know better than to listen to you!"

"After years of driving us all over each summer, yes you should!"

They teased and laughed their way over mountains and through valleys until they reached the Donegal coast where, mesmerized by the view, Larry fell silent. The Atlantic Ocean lay as a silvery ribbon before him, sometimes narrow, sometimes wide depending on the amount of coast between their car and the coastline edge, taunting him, drawing him to her, then disappearing as soon as he started to admire her beauty.

Aidan's car ascended until they'd reached the top of a mountain range. After another series of rises and dips, twists and turns, Aidan pulled into a parking space near the edge of a cliff.

Larry stepped out of the car, in awe. Before him the Atlantic spread as far as he could see.

"She's beautiful, isn't she?" Aidan turned his guest a slight degree to the right. "Here's the real treasure, though."

Larry stared at the sheer cliff before them. Mottled grey and brown, with a bit of tan thrown into the mix, the dramatic rocky display was more stunning than anything he'd ever seen.

"Is all the coast of Ireland like this?"

"No," Aidan answered. "The coastline changes in many ways, sometimes granite like this, sometimes sweeping gently down to sandy shores. The Cliffs of Moher near Galway is our most iconic coastal feature, but this, Slieve League, is to me the most grand."

They left each other in silence then, each alone with his thoughts as they studied the rugged beauty of the Slieve League range.

Aidan took away from the view its enduring strength. Wind and sea had eroded the rocks over time, carving out the landscape before him now, but had not marred its beauty; in fact, their wearing down of the surface had added to its grandeur. He compared that to the strength it had taken him to find his way through the passing of his family. His road was still shaky at times, he would admit to himself if to no one else. If Slieve League could endure storm and time, perhaps so could he.

Larry wondered how many fishermen had stared up at these high cliff walls over time, how many Vikings or other invaders may have tried to scale the edges or sought shelter in the small cove where the cliff curved around to the right.

"Have you noticed," he asked Aidan, "how you can see the wind move the waters below, but you can't hear the waves?"

"It's the height. We're almost six hundred meters, two thousand feet above sea level. In a rough storm you might hear the waves but now, with a lighter breeze, you do notice the silence."

As they returned to their car Aidan told Larry, "Come back over sometime and we can take a boat trip around the base of the cliffs. For now, though, there are other places I want you to see."

Dennis set a glass of wine in front of Fionna at the bar he'd chosen several blocks from the art school.

"Thank you." Once he'd sat down across from her, she asked, "What's this great news you said you had for me?"

"Your recent private showing was very successful." Dennis could not keep from beaming over his new protégé's advancement. "Gallery representatives from San Francisco and London would like to host your work. I'm waiting to hear back from others in Amsterdam, as well as Chicago and here in New York." He raised his glass to toast her. "Congratulations Fionna! You're well on your way to success!"

As much as she'd dreamed of rising in the art world, Fionna could not have imagined how it would feel, the rush inside her, the near giddiness that started somewhere in her heart and rose to her head, a nervous, almost reckless excitement that made her feel she could grab hold of handfuls of stars if she dared reach that high. "Dennis, do you really think so? I mean, these are all possibilities, but will they really come to pass?"

"I know these reps; they've always come through on what they've told me before." As Dennis watched excitement play across Fionna's face, he was captivated most of all by her eyes. Emerald green, always bright, they shone now with more brilliance and light than he had seen in them before. God, she was beautiful. He longed to celebrate with her, not over a glass of wine at a noisy, packed bar, but in his apartment, on the balcony where rattan blinds on both sides would grant them privacy but still offer a view of the stars above and city below. He pictured himself spreading a soft cushion out on the balcony's cement floor, laying a few blankets over it, turning quiet music on and lighting candles for her, then taking Fionna by the hand and leading her down to celebrate her good fortune with all the passion he held inside him.

"Do you know when any of this would happen?"

Fionna's voice broke through his vision; it took Dennis a moment to realize she was asking about the art showings, not his celebration plan. As he cleared his mind, she continued, "Only I have to return home in a few weeks, or I have to update my visa."

"We should go ahead and get your visa extended," Dennis advised. "I don't have exact dates yet for any of this to happen, but you don't want to be shut out of an opportunity because of a visa issue."

I'll have to call Aidan, Fionna thought. If he's not been happy with my being away this long, he'll surely not be thrilled with me being gone for a longer stretch of time.

From Slieve League, Aidan drove Larry to the Connemara region.

"You've seen some of the Connemara marble items I have at home." Aidan pointed to the hills and fields around them. "This is where the marble comes from, the only place in the world you can find it. That's not what I brought you here to see, though."

He pointed to an Irish tri-color flag flying high amidst tall trees. "That's where we're headed."

"We're climbing trees?" Larry teased.

"Very funny! You've been hanging out with me too long, haven't you!"

The gravel road Aidan turned onto had Larry even more curious. After parking their car, they walked a path that led to a small white-washed, thatched-roofed cottage.

"This was Padraig Pearse's summer cottage."

Inside, Larry was guided through a central room with its table, chair, and fireplace, and a bedroom to the left with lace curtains, thick walls, and twin beds. He then followed Aidan to the bedroom at the other end of the cottage. A desk stood at one corner, a washstand and bowl in another. A crucifix hung on a wall next to a bed, on top of the bed a folded tri-color flag had been placed with great care.

Maintaining a respectful, solemn silence, they absorbed the atmosphere of the historical home. Then Larry followed Aidan outside to a bench overlooking a nearby lough, with mountains in the distance. There, Aidan related Padraig Pearse's significance.

"When the British took over Ireland in the sixteen-hundreds, much of the Irish way of life was prohibited: practicing their Catholic faith, owning land, educating their children in parochial schools, speaking their Irish language. By the eighteen-hundreds, between British rule and the famine years, much of the Irish way of life was disappearing.

"Padraig Pearse, among others, wanted to keep the Irish culture, and especially the language, alive. He established a school to teach the language to young people, as well as other aspects of their cultural heritage. He became part of a larger movement to free Ireland from British control. Remember I showed you, in Dublin, the General Post Office building and the Proclamation in the library at Trinity College? On Easter Monday, 1916, Padraig Pearse read that Proclamation outside the General Post Office building, which signaled the start of a rebellion, or rising as we here refer to it. Our poorly armed, largely untrained, rag tag group of fighters were no match for the British Army machine, but they held the British off for almost a week.

"After their surrender, Pearse and the other resistance leaders who had survived the uprising were arrested and swiftly executed. The ideals they planted, though, took root, and several years later Ireland won its independence, except for the six counties of Northern Ireland that have remained part of British holdings."

Aidan gazed out over the lough in front of them. "This location was so special to Pearse. He loved the region, the people, the Irish language they spoke. I imagine his last summer here, in 1915, he knew he and his small army could not defeat the British. I believe he knew he would not come out of the conflict alive. How bittersweet his last visit here must have been, drinking in this view, carrying the weight of a movement on his shoulders, praying for wisdom and guidance before leaving this lough and this cottage behind."

Unable to sleep after her evening with Dennis and their discussion, Fionna tossed and turned until nearly five in the morning, then threw her covers aside and picked up her phone. There was no use putting off any longer the call she had to make.

"Hi, Aidan?"

"Fionna?"

He sounded rushed, Fionna thought. "Am I catching you at a bad time?"

"No. Hold on." Aidan motioned for Larry to take their overnight bags out to the car, and handed his credit card over to the proprietor of the bed and breakfast where they had spent the night to settle their bill. "I'm just checking out of a b&b; I've been showing Larry around some of Ireland."

"Larry?" Fionna questioned, confused.

"Our bus driver from America. Remember, I told you he was coming over for a visit?" Aidan wondered how she could have forgotten when he'd mentioned Larry at least three times in their recent chats.

"Oh, that's right. Where are you now?"

"Leaving Connemara, heading for Donegal Town."

"That sounds wonderful." A sudden twinge pulled at Fionna's heart. Just hearing the names of places she loved visiting made her homesick.

"What are you up to?" Aidan checked his watch. "What is it, five or six a.m. there?"

"Just past five." Fionna's nerves jumped around inside her like mini fireworks exploding. Just come out with it, she ordered herself. Get it over with. "Aidan, I'm not going to be coming home as soon as I thought. Dennis told me there are several galleries interested in showing my works. I might have to spend more time here."

Aidan's heart sank. He could not even paste a false smile across his face as he joined Larry out by their car. "How long?"

"I'm not sure. I'm going to try to extend my visa." Now that she'd broken the initial news, Fionna had to finish the job. "Even when I come home, Dennis thinks I should stay close to Dublin, not way up in Northern Ireland."

Aidan almost dropped his phone. "What?" He demanded so loud even Larry stared at him. Lowering his voice, he turned his back to Larry and the small home they'd just stepped out of. "Who the hell is Dennis to tell you that?"

Fionna forced herself to remain steady and hold her ground. "Things are moving fast, Aidan. I need to be able to meet with art representatives at a moment's notice or fly out in a hurry. Dennis has contacts from San Francisco, Chicago, New York, even London and Amsterdam, all interested in my work. I can't let any of them down by not being accessible."

"Fionna, none of them would expect you to drop everything at a moment's notice. They'd have to give you more time."

"I can't take that chance."

Silence fell between them, heavy with thoughts neither

wanted to express. At last Aidan asked, "How long would you be in Dublin? When would you come home?"

"I'm not sure. I have a friend in Dublin who said I could stay with her until I have a better sense of how this will all play out." Hoping to sway him, she added, "Aidan, this is everything I've dreamed of. You want me to succeed, don't you?"

"Of course I do."

"You've had to sacrifice time with people you care about in order to realize your dreams, haven't you?"

Again, Aidan had to agree, "Yes."

"Then understand I have to do this. Dennis makes sense. He knows the industry better than I do. If he thinks I need to live somewhere where I'll be readily available, I have to listen to that. I can't take a chance on blowing things now. If I extend my visa, I'll be staying in New York. If I can't extend it, I'll be in Dublin. Either way it doesn't mean we won't see each other. It just means I won't be living at your place for a bit."

No matter how she phrased it, Aidan knew the truth in his heart. He also knew he couldn't stand in her way.

"I get it. It's okay. It's all very exciting for you, isn't it?"

Now that she'd gotten over the hurdle of telling Aidan, Fionna allowed excitement to wash her fears away. "It is! I can't believe doors are starting to open for me. I only hope I don't let anyone down."

Aidan drove several minutes in silence, pointing their car north. He drove until they reached a good pullover spot, then parked the car and shut its engine off.

"That was Fionna on the phone," he informed Larry. "She's not coming home, not for a while anyway."

"I gathered that," Larry admitted. "Throws a wrench in your plans, doesn't it?"

"I want her to have all the success she's worked so hard for. I knew it would change our lives, but it's still a hard adjustment."

"It's not a permanent change, right?"

"Probably not."

Aidan sounded unsure. Larry felt bad for him, and even worse that he had no great words of wisdom to offer. The best he could manage was, "Life sends a lot of twists and turns our way, there are no guaranties that our plans are going to work out like we think. Fionna sounds like a lovely girl from the way you've talked about her so many times. If you both truly love each other, you'll end up together someday."

Aidan wanted to believe Larry, but the bus driver's own track record left his words hollow. "You and Christine didn't end up together."

"No, we didn't." Larry allowed his mind to travel back to the states, to the ex-wife, daughter and son who had chosen to build a life without him, not that he could blame them. The fact that he struggled to find a path forward while they were rebuilding their lives apart from him without showing a trace of difficulty made him feel all over again that he was a failure, that they'd made the right choice, they were better off without him. "Christine and I weren't able to make things work in the end. I don't know what will happen with you and Fionna. Just don't lose hope yet. Your story is still being written."

Aidan tried to hold onto the hope Larry talked about as they drove to the final destination on Aidan's mini tour, the town of Donegal.

Donegal Town was busy with the congestion of traffic coming in from several directions all meeting in the center. Aidan navigated his car with expertise, following the flow, the traffic signals, and turnoffs, bearing to the right until he was on the road that led to what he wanted. Arriving at a boxy, angular stone building, he announced to Larry, "Here's the gem I most wanted you to see, Donegal Castle."

"This is a castle?" Larry sounded confused. "It doesn't look like any I've seen in pictures. I thought castles were bigger, with arches and turrets and all."

"Some of them are." Aidan followed Larry's gaze to the building before them. "This one is special. I have two favorite castles, Dunluce, which I'll take you to before you leave, and this one."

Before they entered the building, Aidan went over some of its history. "The original castle was built in the fourteen-hundreds by Red Hugh O'Donnell, one of our legendary chieftains, descended from one of the high kings of Ireland, true Irish royalty. Of the original building, only the stone floor remains. In the early sixteen-hundreds, the Irish rulers, under constant attack from the English, signed a treaty that would bring about peace, but stripped the Irish nobility of their land and power. In 1607 the last of the Irish nobility left for Spain, in effect ending the old Gaelic order, the Irish political and social system. Whether they ever would have mounted a comeback is open for debate, but a comeback never happened."

With that background, Larry followed Aidan inside.

The original stone floor, ancient walls and stairs cast both of their minds back centuries, imagining a lifestyle without electricity, when fishing and hunting would have been paramount in order to feed the people who lived in the castle. Thick stone walls and irregular stairs were built to protect the castle's residents from invaders Aidan and Larry could only guess at.

The second-floor dining hall showed a sturdier grace. Larry could picture kings and rulers, more rugged than refined, hosting dinner parties at the central table, or discussing battle strategies, or warming themselves in front of the grand fireplace on a cold night.

Aidan's imagination settled not on the dinners or discussions that might have taken place in this hall, but on the departure of Irish nobility, and all that was lost when they left. The multiple latticed windows at one end of the hall allowed bright light to shine on the room, yet Aidan felt none of its brightness.

In a display case in one corner, Aidan pointed a book out to Larry. "One of the originals of the Annals of the Four Masters," he explained. "This manuscript chronicles medieval Irish history from the time of the great flood, or Deluge as it's referred to in the annals, to the early sixteen-hundreds. It's a true masterpiece, one of the best collections of Irish history in that timeframe."

Larry admired the volume for the historic piece that it was but was more moved by the emotion in Aidan's voice. "For your favorite castle, this place sure makes you sad."

"It doesn't always." Aidan moved to the bank of windows, focusing on the beams of light flooding through. "I'm sorry. I guess I'm just in a mood."

"Since Fionna's phone call?"

"Aye," Aidan started, then shook his head. "No, it's more than that. Mack hasn't been able to scare up any more bookings for us, the band's not the same without Michael although, God love him, James is really trying. We're struggling to get back in the groove with our music. And now Fionna's leaving, and I want her to succeed, I swear I do, but I didn't think that would mean her moving away."

"Like the Flight of the Earls ended life as they knew it for the Irish, right?"

Aidan nodded. "The Irish people knew they'd lost. They had withstood the Vikings and the Normans, but they couldn't stand against the British. Not physically, anyway. In their hearts and minds the Irish have always clung to independence and to their customs and culture, even when under British rule.

"Those Irish kings fleeing the country knew Ireland was lost. I doubt they truly believed they could regroup and take on the British again. I don't think the Irish people in general had any hopes those old royal warriors could prevail. Their way of life had ended; they had no choice but to accept their fate and rebuild whatever they could of their lives."

The magnitude of the impact the Flight of the Earls and the end of the old Gaelic Order had upon Ireland and her proud, noble inhabitants rose fresh in Aidan's mind. History could not be rewritten, he knew; battles could not be fought again for different outcomes. His ancestors had been forced to take what life had handed them and make the best of it.

"I've learned so much in my visit these past several weeks." Larry's voice carried the same muted tone Aidan's had. "You've talked before about so many of the places we've seen, but seeing them in person, touching real stone, standing on historical ground has a much more powerful impact." He ran his eyes once more over the walls, windows, and furniture around him. "I see now why this place leaves such an indelible mark on you.

"Both our lives are changing. My wife and kids have left me. I can't change that any more than you can hold Fionna back or wave a magic wand and fix what's happening with your band. If your ancestors, though, could hold on through such a huge upheaval of their way of life, I think you and I can find our way through these uncertain times."

Aidan looked once more at the room they stood in, no longer seeing table and chairs, fireplace, and walls. In his mind he saw Red Hugh O'Donnell and the other chieftains gathered around him. He saw the queens, princes, and warriors of old, the fishermen and farmers, hunters and craftsmen descended from them, generations upon generations who had survived hardships he could only imagine. Any difficulties he faced were so much easier than theirs. He owed it to them to straighten his spine, toughen his mind, and move forward.

"You're right," he agreed with Larry. "We will make it through, no matter what lies ahead."

15

Fionna surveyed the paintings spread out along the walls and on the table in the conference room where she and Dennis worked. "I don't know which ones to choose!" She pointed to a series of three Central Park landscapes painted with the smooth technique Dennis had helped her refine. "They should be in the show, shouldn't they?"

Dennis studied the trio through narrowed eyes. "One, maybe. I'm not sure about all three. Setting two aside would leave more room for some of your other pieces."

"Like this?" Fionna motioned to an architectural study, a wide piece on which she had captured both historic and modern city buildings, using more of a rough, textural painting style.

"Yes, that's one of your best." Dennis held up an oval watercolor painting of a large vase of flowers. "Add this. Your watercolor technique is extraordinary, and the soft colors will offset the brighter tones in some of you're acrylic and oil works."

Despite her instructor's assurances, Fionna froze. "What if none of these are what Alicia Conrad is looking for? She'll be here tomorrow! What if I choose pieces she doesn't like? What if I'm not ready for her at all?"

Dennis reached across the conference room table and grabbed Fionna's arm. "You're panicking! Stop it!"

Stunned by the roughness of his grasp, Fionna pulled her arm free and forced down the fears that had risen inside her. "I'm sorry. I'm fine now. What if I'm making bad choices, though? I don't want Ms. Conrad to think I don't know what I'm doing."

"You've shown your work in exhibits before," Dennis pointed out. "That's what got you into our program, how our team discovered you. Prepare for tomorrow's meeting with Alicia the same way you prepared for your prior shows."

"This is different, though. The magnitude of showing my art in a public gallery in New York, where so many more art critics and others will see my works, is not lost on me. It's more important than ever that I show my best pieces."

Surprised by how his star student, who until now had been submissive under his instructions, deferring to any suggestions he made, showed an element of strength in standing up for herself in this selection process, Dennis changed his tone to a more supportive one. "I know you're nervous. You shouldn't be. If Alicia didn't like what she's already seen of your works, she wouldn't be giving you this opportunity. You'll do just fine. Why don't I leave you alone for an hour? I have some calls to make. Go over your pieces again, decide what you think are your strongest works, with an eye toward variety as well as excellence. I'll review them when I return, and we'll finalize your choices."

After Dennis left, Fionna viewed her pieces once again, this time with as critical an eye as she could, looking for strength, imperfections, and variety. By the time an hour had passed, she'd selected ten pieces: one of the Central Park trio, two architectural pieces, the floral vase painting and a companion rose garden piece, portrait pieces of a young dancer who had posed for their art class and an older woman sitting on a park bench, one rough style oil painting of the suitcases and now empty entrance room at Ellis Island, the night scene of lights reflecting off the saxophone player's instrument, and a seascape of Irish waves back home.

Once she'd made her selections, Fionna felt confidence seep back into her spirit. She could see improvements in her techniques, feel the emotional pull of some of her pieces, recognize the variety in her brushstrokes and styles. All of this had been inside her, waiting for release. Dennis had been the one to unlock the door to advancement she had struggled to find. She told herself someday she would paint Dennis a scene of one of his favorite city districts to thank him.

Helen poured Daniel's morning coffee and set it along with his breakfast plate of eggs, potato bread, sausage, and beans before him. She had too much on her mind to eat her own breakfast. All night she'd tossed and turned, wide awake while he slept, knowing what she had to do, fearing his reaction. Now, before he left for work, she had to speak her mind.

"We have to talk."

Daniel nodded, his signal for her to proceed, half listening while he ate.

"You have to set things right between you and Pauline."

Slamming his fork down, Daniel ordered, "I told you, that's a closed book!"

"It's not closed! It's unfinished!"

Standing up to her husband so foreign to her, Helen felt a rush of courage as she continued, "You're hurt by what she's done. Still, she's your daughter. She and Niall are wed now and setting things up proper for themselves and their baby. You know Niall, he's a wonderful man, he'll be a grand husband and father."

"She disrespected my rules. She knew what the consequences would be; she paid that no mind."

"She's still the little girl you taught to ride a bike, to wish on stars. The child whose scraped knees you bandaged and broken toys you fixed."

Daniel wiped his face and hands with his napkin and rose. "I'm off to work. I'll thank you to have no more of this conversation when I return."

Helen slammed a fist on the table, an act so contrary to her both she and Daniel were stunned.

"Either we sort this now, or I'll not be here when you return!"

There! She'd caught his attention! Helen delivered the rest of her message. "You've too long ruled this house with a heavy hand. It's all been your way or none. My fault as much as your own; I've let you have your way. But Daniel O'Shea, I swear with everything in me it stops now.

"You should have been at your daughter's wedding, Daniel. She glowed! She was gorgeous, and so in love with her Niall, and so very happy. Do you remember what that was like? Do you remember our own wedding, the shine in our eyes, our excitement over starting our own new life together, and me three months along with our own first child? Or did you forget that part, that I was in the same way as our Pauline is now? She's not the first girl to find herself in that state. Did you forget your own father washing his hands of you, turning us out as if we were nothing at all? That hurt you so. I could read the pain in your eyes all these years, right up until he, knowing he was ill and not long on this earth, tried to make amends.

"Do you want that same hurt for your daughter?"

For the first time that morning, Daniel looked Helen in the eye. He saw her not as she was now, but as she'd looked so many years earlier, when they were young, newly married, starting out on their own life adventure. God, she was beautiful then. Still was, even if the years had left their tracings on her, faint lines around her eyes now, her hair showing strands of grey. As he studied her, the years of memories he'd locked away fell open. He remembered it all, the pain as well as the joy.

"My God, woman. You're right." Daniel sank back down onto his chair. "I've become like him, haven't I?"

Helen crossed the floor to stand next to her husband, placing a hand of support on his shoulder. "You needn't be. You can turn things around. Start by going to see Pauline and Niall and clear the air between you all."

Dennis found it hard to focus on the paintings Fionna had selected. Her copper hair, tied in a long, flowing braid down her back, shone in the conference room light. Her emerald eyes glistened with excitement. Her cheeks blushed a soft coral rose, matching the ones in her floral vase painting.

He wanted her.

He'd had attractions to other students. Some had developed into short term relationships. Some had been one-night stands. None of them, though, had tempted him as much as this Irish lass did!

Forcing himself to pull his thoughts together and focus on the artwork before him, Dennis nodded approval. "Your selections are good. I don't think I'd change a single one of them. You have balance and variety, color and contrast. Well done, Fionna."

Proud and relieved that he approved of her choices, Fionna asked Dennis, "What's next? I've updated my resumé, made sure all my history is accurate. I've outlined my goals, my art philosophy, all so I can answer any questions Ms. Conrad may have tomorrow. What else do I need to do?"

Dennis would have laughed at her seriousness if he wasn't so concerned with attracting her to him. "Relax," he counseled her now. "You need to relax. Go back to your apartment. Take a nice hot bath. Put on a pretty dress. Meet me at the wine bar at six."

Dennis's ideas sounded wonderful to Fionna. A relaxing hot bath was just what she needed. Back at her apartment, she ran a bath using her favorite lavender bath salts, allowing herself the luxury of soaking in it until the water grew cold. After that she soothed her skin with the lavender lotion she'd brought from home, then brushed her hair a hundred strokes, a habit she'd grown up with, bringing out the deep copper shine. She chose her favorite green dress and tan flat shoes, added dangling copper Celtic knot patterned earrings, and met Dennis at the wine bar near the school.

They drank Chablis, paired with bruschetta, then ate dinner at the Italian restaurant across the street. They talked about art, where it had evolved from, what direction it seemed to be taking next, where they both hoped to take their own personal art projects in the next ten years.

After dinner, Dennis walked Fionna back to her apartment. When she paused at the door to say good night, he insisted, "No, let me go up to your door with you, make sure you're safe."

At her door, Dennis waited while she slipped her key into the lock and turned it to open the door, then stepped inside with her.

Before she could protest, Dennis drew her close and kissed her.

Fionna pushed him away. "What do you think you're doing?"

"Come on, Fionna! How many times have we been out

together this summer? You must have known this was coming!"

"I didn't! I wouldn't have met you tonight at all if I thought you'd do this!"

Dennis tried to put an arm around Fionna's shoulder. When she brusquely brushed his arm away, he got mad. "Don't you think you owe me? That private show a few weeks ago didn't just happen! Your meeting tomorrow with Alicia Conrad, that didn't just come about either! I put myself out there to win those opportunities for you. Now it's payback time."

As he talked, he stepped closer and closer to Fionna, moving her backwards until she was up against a wall. Placing his hands on both sides of the wall behind her, trapping her, he forced another kiss.

"Stop!" Fionna broke into tears. "Don't do this! Please!"

Dennis grabbed her wrists. "You know I can cancel your meeting tomorrow with one phone call! Do you want that?"

Fionna froze. All her hard work, everything she'd dreamed of, came down to this.

She wished she could be virtuous enough to hold her honor intact, force Dennis to leave, and not care one whit whether her career moved forward or ended right now.

She couldn't make that choice.

All the dreams Fionna had ever carried within her, all the years she'd worked so hard to realize those dreams, came to her now.

It's just one night, she told herself. After that she'd have the New York show, then Dennis and all his threats wouldn't matter. She'd be noticed by critics. She would make good contacts. She could move forward on her own after that.

She gave in to what Dennis wanted. After he left, she cried herself to sleep.

"We're off to Dunluce tomorrow. Care to join us?"

Niall shook his head in response to Aidan's question. "Thanks, but Pauline has a doctor's appointment, I want to be there with her."

"Are you sure? Larry will be going home soon."

"I know." Niall felt split in two, wanting to be with Pauline, yet not wanting to miss time with their bus driver friend. "Larry, I'd love to spend more time with you, but you understand, right? You're both coming over for dinner tonight though, aren't you?"

"We were." Aidan nodded to a car pulling into the Donoghues' driveway. "Are you sure you don't have other company though?"

Niall studied the man and woman as they stepped out of their car and approached the house. "Oh my God! That's Pauline's parents!"

"You better go see what they want. Don't worry about us for dinner. You can fill us in on what they have to say later."

Niall hurried across the field and caught the couple before they reached his house door. "Mr. O'Shea, Mrs. O'Shea, can I help you?"

Helen spoke first. "We'd like to talk to you and Pauline."

Unable to read their emotions or purpose, Niall kept his guard up while extending hospitality. "Come in," he offered, holding the front door open for them.

Pauline was shocked to see her parents walk through the door. "Mam? Dad? What are you doing here?"

Daniel took the lead. "We need to talk." Noting the table set for dinner, he apologized, "I'm sorry if we've come at a bad time."

Niall motioned for them to sit on the sofa while he took an armchair across from them, and Pauline the other armchair.

"Your timing is fine. What can we do for you?"

Daniel's eyes shifted from Pauline to Niall and back again. He opened his mouth to speak, then hesitated, as if he'd memorized a speech then found it hard to force out the words he'd rehearsed. At last, he found his voice. "When we first discovered our Pauline was pregnant, we overreacted. I overreacted. I was angry and hurt that you both had disrespected the values we brought Pauline up with. I took a hard stand against your future, but I was wrong. I'm here, we're here, to apologize and to see what we can do to help, with our new grandchild on the way."

Niall would have forgiven and accepted them on the spot, but Pauline, who had been hurt more by her parents' actions, wasn't as quick to forgive. She demanded of her father, "You were so angry with us you wouldn't even attend our wedding. You've hated the thought of this baby. What made you change?"

Daniel covered Helen's hands, folded in her lap, with his own. "My closed eyes have been opened. Severing ties with you both doesn't solve anything; it only adds more hurt. Besides, I've missed out on your wedding, God forgive me; I've no intention of missing out on my grandchild's life."

"Do you mean that, Dad? Only, I won't have us playing a game back and forth over my baby. Either you accept Niall, our baby, and me as is now and never throw this back in our faces ever again, or you leave now."

Daniel studied his daughter. She had her mother's emerald eyes, with the same magic in them, and her mother's smile, but by God she had a touch of his own steel stubbornness as well. She'd do alright for herself, this one, and he'd be on hand to see how her life would unfold.

"I do mean it, daughter. You and your man here are

welcome in our home and our lives. What's past is past."

Niall nodded to Pauline, then stood and crossed the room to shake hands with his father-in-law. "I'm glad this is all behind us." He called to his mother, "Mam, can you set two more places for dinner?"

Fionna avoided Dennis's eyes as she stepped into the conference room to meet with Alicia Conrad. Her hands trembled, her feet wobbled as she walked, but the art critic didn't seem to notice. Ms. Conrad rose, shook Fionna's hand, and motioned for her to take a seat.

"I like the pieces you've selected," Ms. Conrad started in a straightforward manner, relieving any fears Fionna still carried inside her. "I do have one suggestion. Would you replace one of your landscape or architectural pieces with a new still life? It doesn't have to be a fruit bowl! That's a bit overdone, in my mind. Choose something you're passionate about, a stack of books, a musical instrument, a jewelry collection. The subject matter is strictly your choice, but choose something that is meaningful to you. I'd like to see it next week."

Already sorting through and discarding several ideas in her mind, Fionna promised Ms. Conrad, "I can do that."

"Fine." Alicia studied the young woman before her. She may have been nervous, but her eyes shone with a light of … what? Determination? Pride? Alicia couldn't fully place the mood reflected in Fionna's wide green eyes, but found herself drawn to the artist. "Tell me what your goals are, where you'd like to see yourself and your art in, say, ten years."

Yesterday, Fionna had her answer to this question down pat, would not have hesitated a second before replying. Last night had changed everything. Now Fionna took a moment to consider her answer.

"I want success, of course. I'd love to see my works exhibited in galleries all over the world. I want fortune and fame, I'll be honest. But I've come to realize more than that I would like my art to have impact, to make a difference, to represent more of what I stand for and to speak what people might not know how to say.

"I realize the pieces I'm displaying right now don't carry that impact. I'm still learning, and that will be the next focus of my growth in art. I hope an art show in New York can garner enough attention, provide enough interest and contacts that I can take that next step forward."

Impressed with the maturity of Fionna's answer, Alicia assured her, "I have no doubt your show will be successful, and you will realize your dreams. Now, let's go over some of the more specific details."

Fionna departed the meeting excited over how the plans for the show came together. She only hoped she could avoid Dennis as much as possible during the interim.

16

"Turn that thing off! You're taking me out to lunch."

Mack glanced up from his laptop to Kate who had stuck her head around the corner into his office. "I can't, love. I have a number of people I still need to contact."

Kate walked across the floor to Mack's desk and started to close the top of his computer. "And they'll still be there for you to contact tomorrow. You've been at this for days. You need a break, and I need to get away from the house for a bit."

Mack knew when he was defeated. "Alright. Give me five minutes to finish this email, then I'll take you wherever you want to go."

"Paris?" Kate laughed at the shocked look Mack gave her. "Okay, I'll settle for Derry!"

As they drove to town, Kate asked Mack, "Have you gotten any more bookings for the band?"

"No. All the openings I'd hoped for have already been locked up."

"You're good at turning over stones and searching opportunities out. You'll find something."

Mack didn't respond. He wished he had Kate's confidence. All his contacts, though, seemed of little help this time around, and even the secondary markets were harder than ever to break through.

Kate recognized Mack's mood, the set of his jawline, the

seriousness of his eyes, as a time to back off and give him space to sort his thoughts and feelings out. She turned her attention to the scenery outside and let him be.

In Derry, Kate checked in at the dress shop she'd once owned, while Mack stopped in at two of the pubs whose owners he knew. He and Kate met up at their favorite restaurant at the Diamond in the center of the old part of the city.

After reviewing menus and ordering their meals and drinks, Mack asked Kate, "How was the dress shop?"

"Fine. Deirdre's doing a wonderful job with it. How did things go at the pubs?"

Mack shook his head. "No openings. I struck out at both places."

There was a time to sit back in silence, and a time to push. Kate chose the latter now, asking the obvious question she knew was uppermost in Mack's mind.

"How long do you think the band can hold out?"

Mack knew the answer but didn't want to say. Instead, he told her, "I have two or three more leads to follow up on. That might produce some work for the boys."

Kate had no need to point out that "some work" might not be enough.

Mack watched out the window of the restaurant as people and cars passed by, everyday people doing their best to carry on with their lives. He pondered the history of the city, all the struggles it had gone through, how it so often had to push its way forward. How often, he wondered, could he ask Macready's Bridge to do the same?

"I don't know, Kate," he expressed at last. "I'm not sure the boys can take much more. James is young, he'll find plenty of opportunities. Michael has already moved on to another career. Aidan doesn't have any family commitments; he has his studio to build into a proper business and he can continue as a solo artist like he did before. It's Patrick and Niall I'm most worried about."

Kate could feel the pressure Mack carried inside him. She wished she had an answer to offer. "You know the music industry so well. What are the chances things will turn around for the boys?"

"If they held out long enough, things could get better in time. I think we're a good year away from that, though, and I don't think Niall and Patrick can hold out that long."

Mack's face in front of her blurred as Kate's eyes filled with tears. "Oh Mack, I know how hard this is for you. No one could have done better for the boys. It hurts to think of them coming to an end."

"They could surprise me and tell me they'll wait the lean times out," Mack pointed out. "Why don't we give it one more week, let me see if I can get something to break their way. Then we can have them over for lunch or dinner, whatever, and let them make their decisions at that time."

Morning clouds had given way to soft blue skies. "Let's take a walk by the river before we go back home," Kate suggested.

The Foyle's waters sparkled like someone had strewn sequins across their surface as Mack and Kate strolled hand in hand along the walkway. "You know, Kate," Mack said at length, "there's a lot to be said for me not having to work so hard. Imagine all the places we could go and the fun we could have."

It had been months since Kate had seen this romantic, playful side of Mack. She squeezed his hand and laughed, "What did you have in mind first?"

"Someplace quiet." Mack's face brightened as an idea came to him. "For starters, let's borrow Patrick and Moira's wee cottage."

"That would be fun!" As Mack laid out some ideas for their future, Kate's worries lightened, and she found herself looking forward with hope instead of apprehension.

James listened for a third time to the voicemail message his cousin Brendan had left. "Come out to Boston! My band needs a singer. You can share my apartment. You'd love it over here. Call me back."

"What do you think, Da? It would take all my savings for a plane ticket, but maybe it's a chance worth taking."

Mr. McClenaghan pushed more stew on his fork and stuffed it into his mouth. "You've tried the music thing these past few years, and where has it gotten you?"

"Experience, that's what!" James argued back, angry that his father couldn't even be bothered to look away from his dinner and at his only son. "Every time I've gone out, I've learned a bit more about the job, about the industry, about how to keep pushing forward even when it's tough."

"You're chasing pipe dreams, lad. When are you going to wake up to the fact that you'll never make it as a singer? Forget Boston! Work here with me. There's new life springing up across Tory; I'll need help wiring new homes and businesses here. This is where your future lies."

"You're wrong. I see you wearing yourself out day after day with your work. All my life I've heard you swear the next building boom is poised to strike and you'd soon be lining your pockets with gold! That boom never happens. Your ship is still so far from the coast it's invisible! You barely scrape by from month to month, you're skinned half the time, and bone weary at the end of the day. You have no dreams in your heart, no music or hope in your soul. Well, I've had enough! It's Boston I'll be heading for, fighting for my dreams before

I'm old like you! If I fall flat on my face at least I can say I tried!"

James stormed out of the house and down to the end of the road where the cliff edges were most dramatic. This had always been his favorite place to think, as if the waves sweeping in and out of the rocks below him, washing them clean, somehow washed away the debris that cluttered his mind.

The primary thought that ran through him now was whether he was being fair to Mack and Macready's Bridge if he chose to accept his cousin's offer. Mack had taken a chance on him, they all had. Leaving now would put them right back in the position of having no lead singer. Didn't he owe them some loyalty?

On the other hand, a chance to go to America didn't come around every day. He knew his cousin had spent the past two years playing in bands around Boston, he would have a good handle on how to succeed in that area.

Spending what little money he had saved up on an airline ticket, with no cushion to fall back on once he landed in Boston, seemed a huge risk to James. He hadn't saved that money overnight; it would take a good long while to build his savings back up.

What were dreams anyway, though, but a huge gamble? Sometimes one fell flat on one's face in pursuing them. Sometimes one made massive mistakes and had to eat a lot of humble pie in correcting a course gone wrong.

James could either follow his dream, throw all caution aside and give everything he owned and every bit of energy in him into pursuing the success he wanted so badly, or give the dream up once and for all and spend his life following his father's footsteps.

In the end, there really was no choice. James called his cousin, accepted his offer, and then placed a call to Mack.

Niall finished recording expenses on the accounting spreadsheet he had created for the farm and ran the calculations for the month, confirming what he had suspected: the farm was generating a better income than his music was. No matter how long he studied the figures, no matter what angles he looked at them from, the result was still the same.

He couldn't say how long he sat at the desk in the corner of the barn staring at the computer screen. His father's voice breaking through the silence startled him.

"Are we that bad off?"

"We aren't. The farm's doing fine."

"Then why the long face?"

"It's the band, Da," Niall confessed. "We've had so few bookings this year, we're losing money."

Will Donoghue gave his son an understanding look. "And you with a new wife and a baby on the way."

"The timing could be better, right?"

"You've had a few successful years, didn't you invest some of your earnings, or put some aside for days like these?"

Closing his laptop and rising, Niall told his father, "Aye, I had some in savings, but I spent a good deal of that when we remodeled the house. I planned on making that up this year . . .". Niall allowed his voice to trail off.

"Whatever is ours from the farm is yours as well," Will assured his son. "You and your family will always have a home and an income."

"I appreciate that, Da. I just need to decide now about the music. How long do I hold out? How long do I carry on with that?" Always one to face reality and follow a practical course,

Niall thought once again of Pauline, and of the change their lives were about to take once their baby was born. He knew his parents would volunteer to help in any way they could, but they had enough to deal with already. Even if they had the time, he hated the thought of passing his responsibilities for his family off on others. It might be different if the band was pulling in good money; but now, with little to show for their brief time away from home, was it even feasible to stay with the band?

Niall could feel a headache building up, no doubt from too much worry over something he wasn't ready to decide yet. With a smile, Niall turned towards the open barn doorway. "Come on, Da. Let's get some tea and see what kind of pie or pastries Mam's got going. Then we can plan out what tasks we need to line up this week."

Fionna froze at the buzzer for her apartment. If Dennis was coming to call she would not be obligated to let him in, but she was afraid of any kind of disturbance he could create. Whispering a quick prayer for wisdom and strength, she answered the intercom. "Hello?"

"Fionna? It's Alicia Conrad. May I come up?"

Terrified now, sure she was about to lose her New York showing, Fionna buzzed the door open and waited like one waiting for a prison sentence as Alicia's heels clicked up the steps.

"I'm sorry for the intrusion," Alicia apologized, stepping through the door Fionna held open. "I could have called, but I'd rather discuss what I have to in person. I hope you don't mind."

"No, of course not." Fionna's heart sank to the pit of her stomach as she removed from a chair the suitcase she had started packing. "Please, sit down. Can I get you something to drink?"

"No, thank you. I'll get right to the point. Dennis called an hour ago and insisted we dismiss you and look for another student to exhibit at our show." She paused, scrutinizing the young woman seated so nervously in front of her, before continuing. "Have you any idea why he would ask us to drop you?"

"Yes." There was no getting around it. She had to tell the truth. "A few nights ago, after dinner, he made advances, even though I tried to resist."

"You mean he raped you?"

Shocked to hear the word fall so easily off Alicia's tongue, Fionna hesitated. "He would say it was consensual."

"He pressured you into having sex with him though, am I right?"

Ashamed that she had given in to him at all, Fionna struggled to hold back her tears. "Yes."

"Damn him!" The words escaped from Alicia as a whisper, under her breath, not meant for Fionna's ears although she picked them up as if they'd been spoken crystal clear.

"I'm very sorry," Fionna apologized although she had no reason to. "I imagine Dennis could cause a lot of trouble for you. I understand if you need to let me go."

Alicia rose, smoothed her skirt, and reached for Fionna's hand. "Thank you for being honest with me. I assure you we won't be dropping you. Let me handle this. I'll be in touch."

"Last day in Ireland," Aidan announced as Larry entered the kitchen, as if he needed the reminder, as if he hadn't lain awake all night dreading the thought of returning home. "Bet you'll be glad to see the back of me!"

Larry faked a laugh. "Yeah, you've been a crap host all these weeks!"

"I have one day to make up for it, then! I've got breakfast ready for you, then we'll head out."

Aidan pointed his car towards the Antrim Coast. Having started his Irish adventure at Giant's Causeway, to Larry it felt he was now coming full circle. Bypassing the Giant's Causeway site, Aidan drove to the Carrick-a-Rede rope bridge parking lot.

Larry had heard their stories over the past few years of the perils of the rope bridge, particularly of Aidan's penchant for causing the bridge to sway when unsuspecting friends were midway across.

"Oh, no!" Larry insisted. "You're not dragging me across that thing!"

Aidan pulled Larry's arm, forcing him out of the car. "Come on! Your Irish experience isn't complete without crossing this bridge!"

Larry dug his heels in, but Aidan was stronger and pulled him forward. "I don't stand a chance on this, do I?"

"Nope!"

"Alright, on one condition. Don't you dare make that thing sway while I'm on it!"

Making no promises, Aidan led the way down the stairs along the side of the cliff and onto the rope bridge, which was sturdier than Larry thought with its wood and wire planks and wire sides. Halfway across Aidan stopped, set both hands on the side rails, and moved as if to set the bridge swaying.

"Don't you dare!" Larry cried out, panicked.

Aidan laughed so hard he could barely get the word "teasing" out.

The sense of achievement Larry felt when he reached the

end of the bridge and stepped onto the small island it led to was more powerful than any other success Larry had known. He'd faced his fear over the bridge, and now felt he could take on anything that came his way.

After the bridge, Aidan had one more stop to make on their way back to his house. "Dunluce Castle," he informed Larry as they approached the site. "This is my favorite place, the most beautiful castle ruin in all our country."

He led Larry down the long path to the strip of shore where the Atlantic met Dunluce's ground, recalling his last visit here, standing at the water's edge with his father, before Macready's Bridge embarked on their first American tour. How had time passed so quickly, he wondered. It seemed like just last summer they had started their first tour, and now it seemed their time together was over.

He then guided Larry through the ruins themselves, walls of varying heights eroded through time, whispering their secrets to those who wandered through.

"This was quite a risky place to build a castle when you think about it. Right on the edge of the land, here, the views would have been stunning, they still are. It was precarious, though. At one time in the sixteen-hundreds part of the kitchen fell into the sea, and a number of people died.

"Still, it's the most dramatic site you'll ever find in our country, and the best way to cap off your time here."

Aidan left Larry alone for a bit, giving the bus driver time to reflect on the scenery, history, and significance of the castle ruins, while he himself studied the stone walls around him, his mind filled with the echoes of voices of the past. Over the last few years Aidan had forced himself to look forward, not back. He had learned to build a new life after the loss of his family and, thanks primarily to his bandmates, and especially Niall and Niall's family, he'd succeeded pushing past what could have been a crushing grief. Now, though, at the place he'd last visited with his family before their passing, their voices rang in his ears, their faces passed before his eyes like spirits come to pay him a visit.

Along one of the higher walls, Aidan noticed a wildflower had taken root among the crevice where stone met stone, and now trailed down, adorning the structure with delicate pink blossoms. He thought of how, when his heart was broken, new seeds of life had sprung up, how now his life seemed much brighter. He had no idea what would happen with Fionna, if she would come back into his life at all or was gone from him forever. He could not predict what would happen next with his band, whether Macready's Bridge would be able to hold on or whether that was eroding just as the castle walls around him had. He still had Niall and Niall's family though, right across the lough from his house. He had his studio, which would give him something to focus on for the future no matter what else happened.

"It's alright, Da," Aidan whispered into the air around him, sure the spirits surrounding him could hear. "I'm like that vine growing out of the stone. I'll be alright no matter what."

Larry watched the ocean roll in and out and watched gulls and blackbirds circle overhead. He focused on memorizing the combined sounds to replay in his mind whenever he needed once he'd returned home. He ran a hand over the castle ruin's stones, taking their solid feel with him, leaving a piece of his soul among them.

His vacation was nearing an end. The prospect of returning to an empty apartment was as appealing to him as the thought of invasive surgery. The thought of leaving the country where he'd spent the last several weeks seemed just as distasteful.

Larry wished there was a way he could stay longer. He couldn't drive a bus around here, he knew. Even if he could navigate the narrow, tricky roads, Ireland had enough drivers among its own population, they didn't need a middle-aged American pushing his way in among them. Besides, it seemed so far away from his daughter and son; running off to Ireland would widen the separation between them, perhaps permanently.

No, Larry knew he would appear at the airport at his appointed time the next day, board his plane, return home, and carry on, although he knew now part of his heart would remain tied to this land.

"Are you sure you don't mind looking after my works until I get myself situated in Dublin? I'm not sure yet where they should be sent to, and I'm afraid of them being damaged or lost just sitting around some storage place."

"I don't mind at all." Impressed by Fionna's maturity, especially in light of her recent disclosure, Alicia had one more thing to assure her of. "Fionna, I want you to know my art foundation has cut our ties with Dennis."

Fionna hadn't expected that. "You have?"

"Yes. He's brought some wonderful artists our way, including you. I can't stand by any longer, though, and watch him mistreat his female students under the guise of helping them move ahead with their dreams."

"So, he's done this before." Her suspicions confirmed, Fionna knew her decision to walk away from Dennis was the right one.

Alicia felt a wave of shame and regret rise within her. "Yes. I should have taken a stand against it before. I'm sorry I didn't. The one good thing that has come of it, though, is I've had the opportunity to meet you and view your artwork."

She considered the next piece of information she had on her mind, debated whether it would be helpful or detrimental, and decided it had to be shared. "You should be aware that Dennis may try to spread negative information about you."

"Oh no!" Fionna saw her artistic future crash to the ground. "Can he do that?"

"He's done it before. As good as he is at building an artist's career, he can be that tenacious in trying to bring someone down. I'm only telling you this in case you start seeing some kind of smear campaign against you. I don't want you to worry; my name is more powerful than his in this business. I've got your back. You're on your way up, and I'm proud to be working with you."

Fionna rose to leave. "Alicia, I can't thank you enough for the art show ahead of us, for looking after my pieces while I travel home, and for all your support. I'll call you once I'm situated back home and we'll move forward from there."

Michael and Susannah were strolling through St. Stephen's Green when his phone rang. Surprised to see Mack's name come up, he answered the call.

"I heard about your contract being canceled," Mack started out. "I'm sorry about that."

"Thanks." Michael's voice carried a hint of suspicion. Why would Mack even call about that, he wondered.

"James called me last night to tell me he's moving to America." Mack paused, offered a quick, silent prayer, and continued, "I wonder if you'd consider coming back to the band."

"Wow, Mack, that's a tough break for you all."

"It is, although I can't blame him. James has an opportunity there I can't give him with the band struggling as we have been this year."

That struggle was uppermost in Michael's mind as he asked Mack, "Do you mind if I take a couple of days to think about your offer?"

"Not at all," Mack replied. "If you could let me know as soon as possible, though, I'd appreciate it."

"What was Mack's offer?" Susannah asked after Michael had ended the call and slipped his phone back in his pocket.

"James is going to America. Mack wants to know if I'd come back and sing with Macready's Bridge."

"What do you think you'll tell him?"

Michael didn't answer right away. He and Susannah walked along the park's pond, each wrapped in their own thoughts amid the serenity of lush green trees and swans and ducks drifting over the pond's smooth waters. When they came to an empty bench, Michael motioned for them to rest there.

"My dream was always a solo career, Suze. I've made that break, to return to the band now might be a step backwards."

Susannah forced her voice to carry no emotion, not wanting to sway Michael's decision. It had to be his alone. If she persuaded him one way or the other and he regretted his choice later on, he might blame her. "You know I'll stand behind whatever you choose."

"It's a hard choice, Suze. The band has been struggling; even if I went back to them tomorrow, there's no guaranty they'd turn a corner and start pulling in good money again. I'm thinking I can go back to singing at venues around town, the way I used to. I can do voice lessons online, or in schools. I was also thinking, maybe I could collaborate with you on your event planning. You line things up, I can do some of the running, and I can help find entertainment for some of your events. No, I don't mean me, or Macready's Bridge! But I can keep my ears to the ground and scout out worthy acts for your events."

Susannah considered Michael's plan. It made sense to her. It was a risk, but any choice he made would be. "You have good ideas," she told him. "I think you're on the right track. Say no to Mack if you want. We can make it all work."

Larry had returned home. Leaving him at the airport had been bittersweet, each of them knowing they faced empty homes but reminding each other they had the strength to weather their current storms.

To combat the echoes of silence from the rooms around him, Aidan picked up a guitar and started reworking one of the ancient songs he had been experimenting with. When he'd taken the tune as far as he could on his own, he called Niall.

"Are you free to work on one of the songs I told you about the other day?"

"Sure, I'll be right over."

"Bring your pipes and whistles with you."

Niall listened as Aidan ran through the new piece a few times. "Here," he suggested at last, "let's see how I can fit these pipes in."

They tested out various combinations of pipe, whistle, and guitar and had almost reached an arrangement they were both satisfied with when Mack called on Niall's phone.

"Hey Mack, Aidan's with me. Let me put you on speaker."

"I'm glad I caught you both. Can you come out to my place tomorrow? I know it's short notice, but there are some things we need to discuss."

They both agreed they could. "What's up?" Aidan wanted to know.

"James is moving to America. We're down a lead singer again. We need to discuss the band's options."

Niall and Aidan exchanged worried glances. "Is it just me,

or did that sound ominous?" Niall asked after Mack had hung up.

Aidan drew a long breath. "It can't be good if he's in that much of a hurry for us to meet."

Niall sank onto Aidan's sofa. "It seems like everything with the band has been a struggle this year. I don't know how much more we can take."

"It's all part of the business," Aidan reminded him. "We had such a good run right from the start, we were due for a downturn."

"True, but this is more a free fall than a downturn."

"There's no sense dwelling on the dark side. Not tonight. Tomorrow Mack will lay things out for us. It might not be as bad as it sounds now."

Even as he spoke, Aidan knew the truth. The urgency in Mack's voice told the story. Macready's Bridge was in serious trouble. After Niall left, Aidan decided to turn in early knowing the next day, with a trip to Mack's and whatever business that would entail, would be a long one.

He had just turned his bedroom light off and settled in for sleep when his phone rang. Half expecting it to be Niall, he was surprised to see Fionna's name come up.

"Aidan, I just called to let you know I'm in Dublin."

"I thought you were staying in New York until your art show."

"My plans have changed a bit."

"Oh, right. Dennis told you Dublin would keep you connected with the art world if you couldn't extend your visa, didn't he?"

Fionna caught the disdain in Aidan's voice. She couldn't blame him. She'd fairly ignored Aidan while devoting her time to Dennis in New York. "He did say that," she agreed, "but that's not why I'm here. Besides, I'm not working with him anymore."

"No? What happened?"

Blocking as much of the memory of the horrible night from her mind as she could, Fionna only told Aidan, "He turned out to not be everything I thought."

"What are you going to do now?"

"The art show is still on, and I still have goals to move forward with in my art. I'm staying with my friend Carol for a few days until I get myself sorted here." She hesitated, trying to figure out how to broach the next part. "I do have to come out to your place sometime in the next few days to pick up my clothes and belongings ...". Fionna didn't finish her sentence, hoping Aidan would understand what she really was after.

If he did, he gave no notice. "The next couple of days aren't good. Maybe you can come out at the weekend."

The sound of Fionna's voice remained with Aidan long after their call had ended. When he closed his eyes to sleep, her image swam across his mind.

He missed her. There was no pretending otherwise.

She was setting up lodging in Dublin, though. Even as he hated the idea, he had to admit she was right. In Dublin she could visit art galleries, meet with people, and spread her name around far easier than she could if she were stuck out by him. Larry had been right. Fionna had changed, what they'd once had was gone now. She was moving on. He had to do the same.

Aidan tossed and turned all night.

Mack surveyed the three men seated around his patio table. In the years they'd all worked together they had come to feel like sons to him. He felt the pains of a father's heart as he started the discussion they'd all gathered for.

"You all know James has left for America to work in a band with his cousin. It's a fantastic opportunity for him, I don't think any of us can blame him for taking the chance. That leaves all of you, though, in the same place we were when Michael left for his solo career this spring. Before you ask, yes, I've talked to Michael, he feels bad for you all, but he still wants to push for a solo career even though his contract fell through. He'd rather not get locked into a band setting again. So, we're back to where we were in the spring."

Even though they knew this conversation was coming, Patrick, Niall, and Aidan each sat stone-faced while Mack carried on. "Even if we could find a new singer tomorrow, it would take time to fit him in to the point where you all could record and release a new album. You know the struggle we've had trying to book gigs this summer, which should have been our busiest season. I don't think it will be much easier the rest of the year. We need to discuss whether you want to continue, where you're each at financially, if we should carry on, or what you each think you'd like to do."

In the distance, the sounds of Seamus and Kellan barking as they chased each other rang out amid the constant rush of ocean meeting shore at the edge of Mack and Kate's land. Patrick studied the plate of cheese and crackers and fruit before them, took a long drink of coffee as he weighed what was in his heart, then spoke out.

"I have to admit, Moira and I are at the end of our financial rope. I need a steady income at this point. Moira's been patient with me this year, but I don't know that I have it in me to ask her to hold out much longer. Four kids means clothes and shoes, school supplies, food, not to mention the medical bills we still face with Eamon and Eileen."

"I'm on the fence as well," Niall agreed. "I'll soon have a

new baby to care for. As much as I love music, I think working the sheep farm with my father might be the wiser choice, at least for a little bit while I build my savings back up."

In his heart Aidan knew the other two were right, although the truth was still hard to accept. "I have it a bit easier, with no family to support. I'll be honest, I still want us to push through this downturn. I agree with Niall and Patrick, though. They have families to look after, and I can't ask them to hold on any longer just for my sake."

The finality of their decisions weighed each of them down. A heavy silence fell over the patio. Mack gave them time to let their decision settle, then asked, just to confirm, "So, are you saying Macready's Bridge is over?"

"I think so," Patrick admitted. "At least for a little while. We might regroup at some point, but I think we all need a bit of a breather for now. Even you, Mack. You've done an amazing job for us all. But even you must need a break."

"If I'm honest, I have to agree some time away from the pressure of trying to keep things going would be nice," Mack admitted. "I like what Patrick said, though. Let's not call this an end to the group. It's a pause. If you decide anywhere down the line you'd still like to carry on, we can discuss it at that point."

"I remember something my father told me when I first decided to make a living at music," Aidan spoke up. "He warned me it would be a hard road, that for most musicians the lean days would outweigh the bountiful ones, that sometimes I would have to push myself beyond my limits with little to show for it.

"He also said if music was the thing that stirred my heart stronger than anything else, if that's what made my blood race, if that was the dream that consumed most of my waking thoughts, I was almost compelled to chase after it.

"Mack told us once that most bands have a shelf life, they don't go on forever. I don't know if we've hit that point now, if this is the end of our road, but I think we each still carry that dream in our hearts and years on we'll each still be carrying on with music one way or another."

They dined that evening on steaks Mack grilled, with cheesy potatoes, roasted peppers, and wine on the side. As they shared stories, laughing so hard over some their tears flowed, Mack saved all their laughter and words, absorbing as much as he could, knowing even while Patrick and Moira stayed on, he would miss Niall and Aidan as a father misses his children once they grow into adulthood and move on.

"Don't be strangers," he told Niall and Aidan as they rose to leave once the sun had lowered itself to the sea. "Even if the band is over, you're both like family to Kate and me. The door here is always open. Promise you'll stay in touch."

Aidan found it hard to face Mack without the image before him blurring. "You got me through my hardest days, you're like a father to me now. I can never thank you enough for all you've done. If you think you're seeing the back side of me, think again! And you and Kate always have a place at my house any time you want to stay over. I'll expect a good long visit from you once Niall and Pauline's baby arrives."

As the others were saying their goodbyes, Patrick had gone upstairs to retrieve his fiddle. He brought it down, opened its case, fingered its strings, ran his hand over its smooth, worn surface, then turned to the others.

"I know we'll see each other again. I know we'll stay in touch. But Aidan, tonight as you and Niall leave, roll your car windows down. I'll play you home a bit."

Patrick lifted his fiddle, tucked it under his chin, raised his bow, and played the piece his father had taught him.

Aidan drove slowly, he and Niall savoring the sound of Patrick's fiddle carrying over the air, replaying it over in their minds long after they had left Mack's house behind.

Aidan woke to a soft rain falling. The world felt different to him, with Macready's Bridge a closed chapter behind him, the future an uncharted ocean stretched out before him. The myriad prospects ahead of him felt both exhilarating and daunting. He remembered his grandmother always faced decisions over a strong cup of tea. Foregoing his usual morning coffee, Aidan brewed a strong cup of tea, carried it into his living room, lit a fire in the fireplace to chase away the room's damp chill, and stretched out on the sofa to think through his next steps.

He would continue to work on the music he'd heard in his dream. So many fragments of ancient music existed; the idea of giving them new life excited him. In time, perhaps Niall and Patrick would join him on the project. For now, he would create as many updates as he could.

He would have to attempt a dual approach for the months ahead. There had to be small pubs, at least, who might not want to pay the price for hiring a full band but would take a chance on a solo musician. He'd built a decent circuit of repeat bookings once before, he was sure he could do it again especially with his Macready's Bridge experience.

He could now focus on his dream of the recording studio becoming a mecca for musicians, although he continued to need equipment in the carriage house studio. With the way his finances were playing out this year, that dream was going to take a little longer to realize, but he had a wish list for equipment already started.

Aidan finished his tea, then pulled up websites to see what

equipment he could afford. He was so engrossed in his work he didn't hear a car pull in the driveway and jumped when his front doorbell rang. He was even more surprised to find Fionna on the doorstep.

"You said I could come and pick up my clothes," she reminded him in response to his cool look. "Is this a bad time?"

Any time would be inconvenient in his mind, but Aidan supposed she might as well gather her things now, get their breakup over with.

He didn't follow her upstairs, didn't offer her coffee or tea, gave no small talk to delay her task.

As she worked alone, though, downstairs Aidan listened to the sound of her steps overhead and knew in his heart he wanted that sound filling his house again. He wanted to enter a room whose air had been touched by the scent of her perfume. She may have changed while she was in New York, but he hadn't. He still loved her. If she wanted to move on fine, but he'd try one more time to change her mind.

Aidan found Fionna folding the clothes she'd pulled from closet and dresser and laid out on the bed they'd once shared.

"Do you have a couple of plastic bags I could use?" She asked. "I forgot to bring some with me."

Ignoring her question, Aidan asked, "Are you sure Dublin's where you want to be?"

Fionna set the sweater in her hands down and turned to him. "No. I'm not sure of anything right now."

"Then why move there? Why not just stay here?"

"I didn't think you wanted me here."

"I didn't think you wanted to be."

Fionna laughed and shook her head. "Looks like we've both had the wrong end of things."

"Looks like! Let's start over. Fionna, I know your life is different since you went to New York. You can't go there and not have it change you somehow. I still love you, though. If Dublin's where you want to be, that's fine. I'll support that. If you still want to be here though, if you want to be with me, that's what I want as well."

All the time Fionna had been in New York, she'd allowed Dennis to cloud her mind. She'd let her dreams of success turn her head. Somehow, she'd lost sight of the life she'd had with Aidan. The last week, as she broke off contact with Dennis, as she reconfirmed plans with Alicia, Aidan had been the one thing she wanted that she hadn't known how to resolve.

Now Aidan was offering what she wanted most. All the regrets that had consumed her mind and her heart the past several days slipped away. "I want to be here with you more than anything," she admitted.

Aidan crossed the room and took Fionna in his arms. "Then let's get your clothes put back where they belong."

ACKNOWLEDGEMENTS

I would like to thank the following people for their assistance and support in bringing this novel to life:

Ann Crisafulli and Marian Farrant, thank you very much for reading through my manuscript and providing feedback. Your comments were invaluable.

Beth Bales Ostrowski, my cover artist, as always you manage to create just what my mind visualizes. I don't know how you do it, but I am so grateful for you and all you do.

Mark Pogodzinski at NFB Publishing, as always it is a pleasure and honor to work with you. Thank you for helping me realize so many dreams.

Charlie Coughlin, thank you for allowing me to use your fiddle photo as part of the cover for this book, and thank you and all of Crikwater for the music that always carries us home.

Mary Heneghan and The Buffalo Irish Center, thank you for all you do to keep the Irish culture alive in our region.

Tom McDonnell and all at Dog Ears Bookstore, thank you, as always, for your support, and for creating such a wonderful environment for readers, writers, and coffee drinkers, as well as your amazing contributions to our community.

Jack and Maureen Leary Fecio, your friendship and support have always been a warm ray of light. I am so grateful for the empty space at a breakfast table years ago that connected me to you.

I have a wonderful network of friends, and hesitate to mention names for fear of leaving anyone out, but would like to recognize here the following who have long been faithful supporters and encouragers: Kim, Carolyn, Charlene, Linda M, Linda R, Joyce G, Gail, Carol, Ann Marie, Julie, Kelley, Deb, Jennifer, Susan, Judy, Jeanne, Tammy, Danica, Joyce B, Amanda, Elizabeth, Joan, Dave and Sandy, and my sisters, Laurie, Maureen and Roberta. I am grateful to you all.

ABOUT THE AUTHOR

Sinéad Tyrone is a Western New York author with three novels and two poetry collections published. *Walking Through The Mist* and *Crossing The Lough Between*, the first two books in the *Macready's Bridge* series, are set in current day Ireland and cover the crises, challenges and celebrations in the lives of a band of Irish musicians. *Playing Each Other Home*, her current novel, is the third book in the *Macready's Bridge* series. *The Space Between Notes*, a separate novel, deals again with the lives of musicians, this time set in America, and contains a bonus collection of poems that are related to the novel. Her poetry collections, *Fragility* and *A Song Of Ireland*, cover a wide range of subjects, the latter containing poems that relate to her travels throughout Ireland. Her poems have appeared in the anthologies *The Empty Chair, Beyond Bones III*, and *A Celebration of Western New York Poets*. Find out more about Sinéad at www.sineadtyrone.com.

65905530R00129